Praise for *THINGS YOU CAN'T SAY*

"As *Things You Can't Say* shows the gaping fissures that loss and grief can cause in a kiddo's life, so too does it show how those same fissures may begin to heal and close. That we are rooting so hard for their closing in Andrew's life is a measure of how wonderfully real and honest this story is, and of how deep our need is for just the right words."
—**GARY D. SCHMIDT**, Newbery Honor winner and National Book Award finalist

"With grit and authenticity, Bishop takes us inside the head and heart of a young boy. Be prepared to laugh, cry, cheer, and turn the last page with a satisfying sigh."
—**BARBARA O'CONNOR**, author of *Wonderland*

"This touching, authentic novel will open readers' eyes and hearts about mental health issues in loving, 'normal' families. Jenn Bishop explores a challenging subject with sensitivity and grace."
—**BARBARA DEE**, author of *Maybe He Just Likes You*

"People who go away forever. People who come out of nowhere. People who drift away and then drift back. Three years after the death of his father, young Drew finds a way to make peace with all these sorts of people. An emotional tale of a boy who finds it takes equal measures of courage to move forward and to look back."
—**PAUL MOSIER**, author of *Echo's Sister*

THINGS YOU CAN'T SAY

JENN BISHOP

ALADDIN
New York   London   Toronto   Sydney   New Delhi

ALADDIN

An imprint of Simon & Schuster Children's Publishing Division
1230 Avenue of the Americas, New York, New York 10020
First Aladdin hardcover edition March 2020
Text copyright © 2020 by Jennifer Barnes
Jacket illustration copyright © 2020 by Julie McLaughlin
All rights reserved, including the right of reproduction in whole or in part in any form.
ALADDIN and related logo are registered trademarks of Simon & Schuster, Inc.
For information about special discounts for bulk purchases, please contact
Simon & Schuster Special Sales at 1-866-506-1949
or business@simonandschuster.com.
The Simon & Schuster Speakers Bureau can bring authors to your live event.
For more information or to book an event contact the Simon & Schuster Speakers
Bureau at 1-866-248-3049 or visit our website at www.simonspeakers.com.
Book designed by Tiara Iandiorio
The text of this book was set in Adobe Caslon Pro.
Manufactured in the United States of America 0220 FFG
2 4 6 8 10 9 7 5 3 1
Library of Congress Cataloging-in-Publication Data
Names: Bishop, Jenn, author.
Title: Things you can't say / by Jenn Bishop.
Other titles: Things you cannot say
Description: First Aladdin hardcover edition. | New York : Aladdin, 2020. |
Summary: Three years after his father's death by suicide, twelve-year-old Drew
embarks on a journey toward understanding, forgiveness, and hope.
Identifiers: LCCN 2019006194 (print) | LCCN 2019011254 (eBook) |
ISBN 9781534440999 (eBook) | ISBN 9781534440975 (hardcover)
Subjects: | CYAC: Loss (Psychology)—Fiction. |
Suicide—Fiction. | Fathers and sons—Fiction.
Classification: LCC PZ7.1.B55 (eBook) |
LCC PZ7.1.B55 Th 2020 (print) | DDC [Fic]—dc23
LC record available at https://lccn.loc.gov/2019006194

FOR MY LIBRARY TEENS—FROM MALDEN,
CONCORD, CARLISLE, AND HOMEWOOD.
AND FOR AUTUMN, WHO BELIEVED
IN THIS STORY FROM THE BEGINNING.

EVERYONE'S GOT A FAVORITE COLOR.

A favorite book, band, movie. But what about a favorite sound? For me, that's the easiest: little kids laughing. A four-year-old absolutely losing it because of something funny I just said? No better sound in the universe.

That's the thing about little kids. They don't know how to fake it yet. There's nothing they're hiding beneath the surface. No tricks, no secrets.

I've got my head ducked down below the library's puppet stage in the corner of the children's room, right by the new picture books, and I'm using my very best performer voice. "Zombie Goldilocks thought Papa Bear's bowl of brains was too hot." With my right hand, I make the zombified Goldilocks puppet spit out brains in every direction. "Pttew. Pttew."

The little kids giggle. One of them maybe even snorts.

"But Mama Bear's bowl of brains was too . . ." I wait for one of the kids to chime in.

"Stinky!" a girl in the front yells out—I think it's Claire, but I can't tell for sure with my head ducked down. The other kids around her laugh and laugh.

I stick my head up for a second and catch the children's librarian, Mrs. Eisenberg, smiling in her rocking chair, just past the rainbow rug the kids are sitting on.

"Her brains were too stinky. Pee-yew! But then Goldilocks found Baby Bear's bowl of brains, and it was . . ."

"Just! Right!" they yell out together.

Smiling makes it hard for me to do this voice, so I try super hard to keep a straight face.

Now, it's one thing to zombify Xander's bedtime stories. Of course my brother's going to find it funny.

But I didn't know how well it'd work for other kids until that time last summer when Mrs. Eisenberg asked me to fill in for her. But afterward she said that if I wanted, I could do it more often. She said it showed *ingenuity*. Whatever. All I know is it makes the kids laugh. And that it's the kind of thing Dad used to do for me when I was little. Of course *he* was good at telling stories. Wasn't that what he was doing the whole time? Our whole lives a big fairy tale, him pretending everything was perfect—fine—when obviously it wasn't.

There. Now the smile is gone.

"When Papa Bear came home, he saw the empty bowl. 'Now, who ate my brains?'"

I peek again and catch Demaris in the front row, picking his nose. I push Papa Bear out like he's going to leap off the stage. "Was it you, Demaris?"

Demaris's finger flies out of his nostril so fast. "Noooooo!" He giggles.

"Was it . . . Abigail?"

Shy Abigail's lips are zipped.

"It was you, wasn't it? It's always the quiet ones. I'm onto you."

For the past two weeks, I've been trying different ways to get her to participate, but each time, no dice. *Come on, Abigail.*

"Nah," I say. "You're right. You're not a fan of brains. Your favorite food is probably more like . . . hmm . . . boogers?"

"No, it's not," Abigail says. "It's pizza!"

"Well then, who on earth came in here and ate all my brains?"

The kids crack up. For a second, I sort of feel for the dude. If someone barged into my house and ate all my favorite food, I'd probably be annoyed like Papa Bear too.

As I'm finishing up with "Zombie Goldilocks," Mrs. Eisenberg mouths that she's heading upstairs. I nod to show her I have things under control down here and reach for the Little Red Riding Hood puppet that I turned into a vampire.

"Once upon a time, there was a liiiittle vampire . . ." The kids stop fidgeting the second I show them Little Red with her painted-on fangs.

By the time I'm wrapping up the story, all the moms and dads and babysitters have come down with their coffees and warm cookies from the new café upstairs, ready to take their kids home for naps and lunch. I'm picking up half-scribbled-on coloring sheets left on the tables when all of a sudden I catch something out of the corner of my eye. A girl. She's about my age, with short blond hair that ends at her chin and bright red glasses. She's sitting at one of the tables. When'd she come down here?

I walk over to her. "If you're looking for the teen room, it's upstairs. You take a right past the café and it's—"

"I'm not looking for the teen room," she says. Her voice is quiet and it's only when she opens her mouth that I notice how frowny it is.

I glance back at the puppet stage. Did she come in while I was doing the show? Wait—tell me she wasn't listening when I did that insane grandma voice in Vampire Little Red Riding Hood? I'm half-ready to dart behind the puppet stage and never come out again.

The best part about the children's room is that no one my age ever comes down here. Not since they put in the teen room upstairs and the café across from it. Down here I'm safe.

Just then the elevator door opens and out comes Mrs. Eisenberg holding a large stack of cardboard boxes that looks like it's about to topple over. I hustle to help her before the boxes fall to the ground.

"Thanks, Drew. Always coming to my rescue." Mrs. Eisenberg beams at me.

As we're putting the boxes down next to her desk, Mrs. Eisenberg spies the girl who overheard my whole story-hour routine. "Oh my gosh!" She laughs. "You startled me. Audrey, right?"

The girl—Audrey, I guess—nods.

"I almost forgot all about you, Miss Audrey. I see you've met our Drew. He's been helping me out in the library for the past three summers now."

Audrey gives me a funny stare and it's like I can read her mind. I know what she's thinking—there's got to be something seriously wrong with a twelve-year-old boy who chooses to hang out in the library's children's room all summer.

"Audrey's going to be working with you this summer, Drew. Her family just moved to town and her mother's up in circulation. Janet, isn't it?"

"Yup."

I don't care who Audrey's mother is upstairs. I

need to rewind to hear what Mrs. Eisenberg just said. Someone else *my age*? Working down here? With me? For the whole summer?

"Drew, can you show Audrey how to cut out name tags so we can get ahead for the rest of the week?"

"Suuuure."

Audrey shuffles behind me as I point out where Mrs. Eisenberg keeps all the different colors of construction paper, plus the stencils and scissors, and where she taped up a chart showing which name tags go with which theme for story hour.

"That all make sense?" I ask.

"It's cutting out name tags," she mutters. "Not exactly rocket science." Under her breath she adds, "I can't believe they stuck me in the *children's* room."

What I want to say is, no, of course it's not the *best* part of helping out in the children's room. But sometimes when the little kids have been screaming their heads off all morning and you get a few minutes of peace and quiet, it's kind of nice just to sit and cut. It's easy. You can't mess it up.

But I can't say any of that, and definitely not to someone I barely know who doesn't exactly seem to have a great attitude, so I just shrug, grab the yellow paper and the sun stencils, and walk back over to the table where we'll be working together until lunchtime.

A woman pushing a fussy red-faced baby in a stroller steps off the elevator.

Audrey sits down at the far side of the table from me, eyeing the baby suspiciously.

Normally I'd say hi to the mom and wave at the baby, but it feels weird to do any of those things with Audrey here. Almost like I'm being watched.

Eventually the lady grabs a few picture books and leaves just as the baby starts wailing, and for a few minutes, we *snip-snip-snip* in the quiet. Mrs. Eisenberg softly flips through the pages of one of her library magazines. The loudest sounds are the hum of the aquarium and that one light above the astronomy books that always buzzes even though the janitor keeps saying he's going to fix it.

Until Audrey starts sighing—each time she cuts out a sun, she clicks on her phone to check the time. Sigh. Yawn. Click. Sigh. Yawn. Click.

If her goal is to see how slowly time can pass, she certainly figured out a solid method.

Tap-tap-tappity-tap. Mrs. Eisenberg starts typing on her computer, then groans. "Not again."

Across from me, Audrey perks up. She sets the scissors down on the table and jogs over to Mrs. Eisenberg. "Do you need some help?"

"Any chance you're good with computers?" Mrs. Eisenberg chuckles.

"I started the robotics club at my last school." Audrey takes over Mrs. Eisenberg's seat. "I think you can say I'm good with computers."

Click-click-clickety. "Oh man. Your browsers are really out of date. Does this thing freeze all the time?"

"Depends on your definition of 'all the time.' I keep asking our IT lady—Ellie—to come take a look at things down here, but I've got to be honest with you, Audrey, we're all working on ancient machines. Upstairs, downstairs, you name it. There's just no money in the budget to replace them."

"You don't need money to update your browsers. I mean, yeah, you can get nice machines with money. But I can help you upgrade a lot of this without it costing anything."

"You can?" Mrs. Eisenberg glances back at me and I accidentally drop my scissors. "Isn't this great, Drew?"

I fumble for them and start to cut again. "Yeah," I mutter. "Great."

Mrs. Eisenberg leans over Audrey, following whatever she's doing. Or more likely trying to follow.

Who does Audrey think she is, anyway? Does she really think she's going to fix all the library's computers? She's twelve. Or thirteen? Actually, I don't know how old she is. But I do know how the library works, or at least how it used to work.

There are some things I don't get to do. Like putting away all the books. That's the job for the teens—the pages. I only get to do those things if they're out sick and the librarians really need help. And the computers? That's Ellie's job. You can't just come in here and take someone else's job. It doesn't work like that. Even if you're—*especially* if you're—just a kid.

"Audrey, this is amazing! We didn't know what we were missing down here. You're going to be a really wonderful addition to our team, you know that?"

Audrey gives Mrs. Eisenberg back her chair. I glance down at my cutting and realize I've totally butchered my sun. I crinkle it up and toss it in a nearby garbage can. It misses.

When Audrey sits back down at the table across from me, there's this new smile on her face. She doesn't

even reach out to her phone to check the time again, just grabs a new sheet of paper and starts tracing.

Snip, snip, snip.

Clickety-click-clack.

A few minutes later Mrs. Eisenberg comes over to our table. When I look up, Audrey's got her suns placed in perfectly neat little piles. Wait a sec. How'd she finish almost twice as many as me?

"Looking good! You know, Audrey, I was just thinking how a lot of parents have been inquiring about STEM programs for the little ones, but I don't have a clue where to start. Is that something you'd want to help me with?"

For the little ones. She doesn't mean in place of story hour. Wait, does she?

"That sounds fun," Audrey says. "Just the planning, though . . . right?"

Mrs. Eisenberg beams. "Fantastic. It'll take some time to get it off the ground. Well, I should probably take advantage of the quiet right now and pop upstairs for a bit. You two holler if it gets too crazy or send one of the pages up for me." Sometimes I forget they're even down here. The teens who pick the requested books off the shelf or reshelve the returns

are so quiet—honestly almost ninjalike sometimes. Plus, they're always wearing headphones.

I glance at Audrey, who's somehow managed to churn out perfect suns even while talking, like she's some kind of multitasking machine. Jaw clenched, I start tracing again.

By the time the church bells across the street ring for noon, I'm shooting out of my chair and over to Mrs. Eisenberg, asking if I can take an early lunch. I grab my sandwich from the staff fridge and use the last seventy-five cents in my wallet to get a candy bar from the vending machine.

If I'm going to have to suffer through an entire afternoon of Audrey trying to show me up, I need some sugar, stat.

Upstairs, I pass by Mom at the reference desk and give her a little wave, but she's busy with Mrs. Kaminsky from down the street and barely able to wave back.

Once I'm outside, I settle onto my favorite bench under the tree. Half in the shade, half in the sun. No Audrey. No screaming babies. It's so perfect I'm almost suspicious. I bite into the Snickers—my favorite—

and let the chocolate and peanuts quiet my rumbling stomach.

Audrey rounds the corner, earbuds in. I stop chewing. If I stay as still as possible, maybe she won't see me. She sits with her back against the brick library wall, her head drooping forward as she pulls a book out of her bag.

In the clear!

I return to chewing. Maybe the smart thing would be to run away—scram while she's deep into her book. But I can't let her take over all my spaces. Not that quickly. I've got to stand my ground somewhere.

Audrey sniffles.

No. Please. *Don't cry. Don't cry. Don't.*

Oh no. She is. She's crying. Her hands shoot up and cover her face, but it's happening. It's happening and I'm right here and now I definitely can't run away. You can't run away from a crying person. She swipes a hand under her nose and then—*spotted.*

"What?" Her lip quivers as she shoots me—*me*—a withering stare. What exactly did I do wrong here?

I hold up the candy bar. "Do you want a piece?"

Audrey scoffs, "Of the candy bar that you've already taken a bite out of?"

I sigh. Why did I for one second think it was a good idea to offer in the first place? "I was gonna break a piece off the other side, but fine, if you want to say no to free chocolate, that's—"

"Fine. Sorry. I—" Audrey exhales. "I guess I'll have a bite."

I rip off a chunk from the other side and hand it to her, still in the wrapper so it's free of Drew germs.

I'm not even sure why I'm doing it. Actually, that's not true. I know exactly why I'm doing it: because it's the kind of thing my dad used to do. He said a little bit of chocolate always made people feel better. Not exactly what you'd expect to hear from a dentist, right?

A piece of chocolate goes down the wrong way, and I need to sip some water to keep myself from coughing.

Audrey chews quietly while I get my coughing fit under control. "Did you ever have to move?" she asks.

I shake my head.

"You're lucky, then. I've had to move five thousand times, and each time it sucks more than the last."

I take another bite of the Snickers. "Why do you have to move all the time?"

"My dad's a physicist. He got this new job at Brown, which, supposedly"—she crosses her fingers—"is the job he'll have for the rest of his life. If he gets tenure. But that's what they said about his last job, so who knows."

"Where'd you live before?"

"Let me see." She counts on her fingers. "Palo Alto. Santiago, Chile. Austin, Texas. Chicago. Pasadena. And now here."

"Five *thousand*, huh?" I joke.

Audrey sticks her tongue out the side of her mouth. There's a little bit of melted chocolate on it. "Whatever. At least your dad stays in one place."

She hit that one right on the nose.

"What's your dad do, anyway, that makes your family have to live in *Rhode Island*?" She says it as if there are rats and cockroaches swarming all around us. It's the ocean state, Audrey. Not the sewage state. Sheesh.

The truth catches in my throat, like it has for the past three years. That Dad doesn't *do* anything anymore. He stopped being anything at all—my father, a Little League coach, a storyteller, a dentist, everything—when he killed himself. "He's a dentist."

"And he lets you eat candy bars for lunch?"

She doesn't notice my lie. Skips right over it. Maybe I've gotten so good at pretending everything's okay now that I fool her, too.

"I have a sandwich!" I raise the plastic baggie up in the air.

Talking about Dad like he's still around is starting to seriously weird me out, so I switch subjects real fast. "What grade are you going into?"

"Seventh."

"Me too. You going to school in town?"

"I'm on the waiting list for Moses Brown."

"Oh."

"It's a private school." Audrey reaches for her earbuds.

I know it doesn't entirely make sense, but for some reason I still want to talk to her. It would be nice to get along with the person I'm going to be spending all my summer weekdays with. "Hey, what were you listening to?" I ask.

"Puccini," she says, rubbing one of the earbuds between her fingers.

"Is that some new band?"

Audrey snorts. "Are you serious?"

"I'm going to go with *no*?"

"Puccini is opera, Drew."

Opera? What seventh grader listens to opera?

And just like that, Audrey pops her earbuds back in and pretends I don't exist. I try to do the same, but if I'm going to be totally honest, it doesn't work. Whether I like it or not, I have a feeling I'm stuck with Audrey for the rest of the summer.

THWUMP. THE BALL FILIPE PASSES

hits me square in the chest, then bounces down the driveway. Wiping sweat off my forehead, I scramble after it, snagging it just as it reaches the rhododendron bush by his front door.

"What—you thinking about some girl? Willa again? I told you, no way is she going to be interested in either of us. Time to give it up, Drew."

I dribble the ball a little bit and go in for a layup. The ball swishes through the net and I catch it in my other hand.

"No . . ." I laugh and bounce-pass back to my friend so he can take a shot. "Not Willa."

"Someone else?" Filipe's eyebrows shoot up as he dribbles the ball in place.

"*Not* like that. Trust me. Just—there's this new girl at the library. Audrey. She—" It's hard to pinpoint what exactly it is about Audrey that drives me nuts. It's everything about her. How she clearly doesn't want to be there—thinks she's too good to work at the library—yet at the same time she's totally kissing Mrs. Eisenberg's butt with all the techie stuff. "She's just . . . the worst. I asked her what she was listening to, right? And it was opera. Opera!"

"Well, she does hang out at the library. What'd you expect?"

I shoot Filipe a look. He's been making little jabs at my library gig since school let out.

The thing is, the library is supposed to be *my* place. That first summer after Dad died, Mom signed me up for summer camp at the Rec. Same one Filipe and I had been going to since we were in kindergarten. But every day, I barely made it through the first half hour before I lost it—I'd puke—and Mom had to come pick me up.

It wasn't that I was actually sick. It was more like after what happened with Dad, I couldn't handle being away from my mom. Didn't really trust anyone anymore. How could I? Camp was eight hours long, but those eight hours felt like eight years. I'd done story hour with Mrs. Eisenberg when I was little and she told Mom she didn't mind watching me. There were plenty of other kids whose parents "took advantage" of her already, and I wasn't half as much trouble as they were.

Mom probably thought it'd just be for a week. That after a few days with an old lady like Mrs. Eisenberg, I'd be dying to be back at camp with all the other kids my age.

But I wasn't. I loved hanging out down there, helping with the little kids, knowing that Mom was just upstairs. For the first time since Dad died, I felt safe. A few days turned into a week, turned into three summers now. Mrs. Eisenberg says she can start paying me next summer as part of the page-in-training program.

But now, out of nowhere, I've got this Audrey girl all up in my space. What if Mrs. Eisenberg thinks her STEM program is more exciting than my zombie story hour? She wouldn't take that away from me . . . would she?

"Drew! You think I can make this one?" Filipe is halfway up a tree at the edge of his yard, but somehow he still has the basketball in one hand. How does he do it?

"Um . . . no."

This is how it's always been. Filipe thinking he can do ridiculous stuff, and then falling on his face. But ever since he made the U13 soccer team earlier this year, it's like he's got superpowers. At least when it comes to sports.

How'd he suddenly get so strong and so . . . good?

"Let's see!" Filipe shouts down at me.

He won't have enough momentum. No way. Not with his legs clinging to the tree. He thrusts the ball toward the net, but it dips too low too fast and bounces on the pavement, heading for the open garage.

I've just snagged it from beneath Mr. Nunes's workbench when I hear a motorcycle.

Thrum thrum. Thrumthrumthrumthrumthrum.

Did Filipe's older brother, Anibal, get a bike? It sputters as it comes to a stop, but it doesn't pull into Filipe's driveway as it slows down. It pulls into mine.

Filipe's staring at the thing with his mouth open. "Nice ride."

I give the ball a few bounces and watch as the man props up his motorcycle. He removes his helmet and carries it over to my front door. Is he lost? Maybe he's one of those people who goes door-to-door selling stuff. Or trying to save the environment.

Mom left a little while ago to pick up Xander from his friend's house, so there's nobody there to answer the door. I stop bouncing the ball. "Come on," I say to Filipe.

"You want to go over there?"

"Yeah," I say. For a second, I forget that Filipe doesn't get it. Without my dad now, I'm the second most in charge. At his house, he's got Anibal and his mom and his dad. Filipe's never had to be responsible for anything. "What if he's trying to case the house?" Okay, not super likely, but it could happen.

"Drew, be serious."

"You never know."

We have to wait at the edge of his driveway forever while some lady on her cell phone in a Prius slowly creeps up the street.

"He's probably just lost," Filipe says.

Finally the Prius passes us and we dart across the street. The truth is, when my mom isn't home, I'm not supposed to answer the door. For the past two years, she's let me stay home alone—*finally*—so long as I follow that rule. But Mr. Chapman next door is out watering his garden, so I think we're in the clear.

"Can I help you?" I ask the man loudly, standing my ground.

The motorcycle guy turns and slips his sunglasses up onto his hair. It's curly brown, but with the littlest bit of gray at his temples. If I had to guess, I'd say he's probably around my mom's age—early forties. Yeah, he's definitely too old to be going door-to-door to save the environment. "Drew, right? I'm Phil." He reaches out his hand, like this is the right time and place for a handshake. He's smiling at me like he knows me, but I've never seen the dude before in my life. So how does he know my name?

I keep my hand right where it is and flash Filipe a *Who is this guy* eyeball. Filipe only shrugs.

"Look, I think you've got the wrong house or something," I say, ignoring the fact that he somehow knows my name. I'm starting to wish we hadn't come over here in the first place. Maybe if we'd stayed across the street at Filipe's, he would've rung the doorbell, waited a minute, and just left.

He slips his hand into the front pocket of his jeans. They're all beat up and worn, not at all like the jeans my dad used to wear.

"I'm sorry, Kayla—your mom, she didn't . . ."

Wait. This guy knows my mom? From where?

He's still staring at me, like he expects me to figure this out myself. I glance at Filipe, but he looks as confused as I probably do.

"Oh, jeez." He runs his fingers through his hair and pulls his cell phone out of his pocket. "My phone died on the road. The plans changed and I decided to swing up through Rhode Island first and . . . what am I saying? You don't even know what I'm talking about." He takes a few steps toward his motorcycle. "I'm real sorry for throwing a wrench in everyone's plans. When's your mom supposed to get back, Drew—wait, is that short for Andrew?" There's this weird look on his face all of a sudden, almost like he wants to smile but he's stopping himself.

"Yeah," I say. The second it comes out, I regret it. Why does he need to know? And what's he talking about? Plans? He and my mom, they made *plans*? Since when?

"You know what? I saw a coffee shop back a little

ways. I bet they'll let me charge my phone there. Tell your mom I stopped by, all right? I'll give her a call."

He has her phone number?

"Okay . . . ," I say. He's already on his bike, revving it up. "Wait," I shout. "What's your name again?"

He shakes his head like he can't hear me.

"Your! Name!" I shout again.

He cuts the engine. "Sorry," he says. "It's Phil." And then he revs it up again.

Filipe and I just stand there, watching as his motorcycle heads back down our street.

It's only as he leaves that I realize I've been clenching my stomach the whole time.

"I DIDN'T KNOW YOUR MOM HAD A

boyfriend," Filipe says as we walk back toward his house.

"A *boyfriend*?" I choke on a laugh. "No way." I've never seen that guy before in my life. Besides, Mom would tell me if she had a boyfriend.

The couple times she went out on dates earlier this year, trust me, you couldn't miss it. She emptied out her whole closet on her bed trying to figure out what to wear. The upstairs reeked of perfume.

Each time, she sat Xan and me down beforehand

to let us know where she was going and all the details. But that was it. A first date, never a second. All that fuss for nothing. She says online dating's way harder than it looks in the movies.

No, there's no way she could be dating that guy. Not in a million years. For one, she's always around in the evening. When would they have even been on a date?

Maybe he's some patron from the library who's got a crush on her. Honestly, the more I think about it, it's the only thing that makes any sense. He must've overheard her talking about me one day at the library. And then looked up our address online. It's super creepy. Like, stalker-ish, really. It's a good thing I had Filipe there as backup.

Next thing I know, Filipe's trying to twirl the ball on the tip of his finger like he's the newest Harlem Globetrotter. I snatch it real fast, and then we both dart across the street, playing one-on-one like nothing happened. Like some strange guy on a motorcycle didn't just stop by my house looking for my mom.

It's not until Mrs. Nunes lays on her horn so she can squeeze past us and into the garage that I remember I still need to take out the chicken to defrost for dinner. She gets out of the car, their old husky, Tobey, climbing out after her. I still can't believe she gets to take Tobey to work with her. Maybe I'll be an architect when I grow up if it means I can bring a pet with me every day.

Tobey heads right for me, his snout sticking up in the air. "Hey, Tobes." I pat his head and give him a good scratch around the ears. "Hey, Mrs. N."

"Nice to see you, Drew." She asks Filipe, "How's that free throw coming along?"

"Fine."

I toss the ball to Filipe, who takes a shot to demonstrate. The ball bounces off the rim.

"I made ten in a row earlier," he says. "I swear."

"I'll bet you did." Mrs. Nunes whistles for Tobey. "Come on, Tobes. Let's go get supper ready."

I wipe some sweat off my forehead, remembering the chicken again. "Be right back," I shout, jogging down the driveway.

"Huh?"

"I've got to defrost the—never mind. I'll be back in like five seconds."

Filipe mutters something under his breath. It sounds like he says, "Whatever."

Whatever, Filipe. The chicken can't exactly defrost itself.

Back home, I take the chicken out of the freezer and place it in a glass dish to defrost in the refrigerator. I'm pouring myself a glass of water when I hear stones skittering on the side of the driveway.

The front door bursts open, and in shoots my little brother, making a beeline for the bathroom. "I have to pee! I have to pee! I have to peeeeee!"

Someday Xander will stop announcing every bathroom visit, but today is not that day.

Mom comes in behind him. "Hey, hon." She ruffles my hair. "Gosh, you're sweaty. Do you want to take a shower before we get started on supper?"

"This guy stopped by while you were gone," I start to say, when Xander zooms around the corner and flings open the fridge.

"Mom, I need a snack!"

"How about some carrots and hummus?" Mom says.

Xan scrunches his nose up at *hummus*. "How about some cookies?"

Mom shakes her head at him. "Not this close to dinner, bud. How about . . ." She rummages through the fridge. "Sorry, Drew. Can you say that again? Someone stopped by? Did he leave a name?"

I didn't know your mom had a boyfriend.

My stomach clenches again as I try to remember exactly what he said. He got all flustered. And he said something about plans changing. Plans, like . . . a date? No way, though. He definitely wasn't dressed for a date. Not with those ratty jeans.

"Who do you know who rides a motorcycle anyway?"

Mom jerks her head, banging it against the inside of the fridge. That has to hurt. She rubs at it while handing Xan a string cheese, and reaches for her cell phone on the counter. She types something in and presses it to her ear, rubbing that spot on her head with her other hand.

"Do you want an ice pack?" I open the freezer, looking for the soft kind Mom uses when Xan or I hurt ourselves.

When I spin around, she's already put her phone down and now she's at the sink filling up one of the biggest pots. The kind she only uses when we're having pasta for dinner.

"But what about the chicken?"

She adds a dash of salt to the pot and *click-click-click*s the gas on beneath it.

Okay, she must have *really* hit her head.

"Mom?"

She doesn't answer right away.

"Mom, who was that guy?"

It's not until she turns around that I can finally see her face. She's doing the same thing that guy on the motorcycle was doing, that same thing with her mouth. Like she wants to smile, but she's stopping herself from doing it. Who stops themselves from smiling? Who smiles like that after they just whacked their head?

"This isn't how I planned to tell you," she says. My stomach goes all tight again. I can't believe she kept this from me. Filipe was right.

"Are you . . . dating him?"

"No." Mom shakes her head. "Not at all, hon. I haven't seen Phil in years." She pulls up a chair at the table and gestures for me to take the other one. "He's an old friend of mine from high school. He put out a call on Facebook for places to crash as he makes his way across the country on his motorcycle. Things got all turned around and he's swinging into Rhode Island a little earlier than expected."

"He's going to stay *here*? In *our* house?"

Mom tucks a strand of hair behind her ear. "Yes,

Drew. We're only talking a few days. We've had my friends stay here before. Remember when Laura came out for Thanksgiving last year?"

That's different, though. Laura's a girl. Plus, I'd met her before. She's not some random guy just appearing at our house one day, no advance notice, no nothing.

"I can see how it must have been confusing for you to have him stop by before I told you, and I'm sorry about that. But sometimes things just don't go according to plan, right?"

Xander runs into the kitchen. "Drew! My show stopped. Can you fix it?" I don't exactly have a choice—Xan practically drags me into the living room.

I glance back at Mom, trying to make sense of what she just said as Filipe's words ring through my head. Her explanation doesn't entirely add up, though. Not really. There's something different about Mom, something that changed the moment I mentioned that guy. I just can't put my finger on what.

Reaching up above the TV in the living room, I reboot the wireless. It takes a minute, but then Xander's show starts playing again.

"You're welcome," I say.

My brother's eyes are glued to the screen. I swear I stop existing once the TV is on.

When I'm back in the kitchen, Mom asks, "Can you grab some spinach from the fridge?" I hate how she says it like everything's okay, like there's nothing messed up at all about this perfect stranger suddenly joining us for dinner.

Why didn't she say something before? When she first knew he might come? If he's really just a friend like Laura, she would. No, she's not telling me everything. I don't know why, but she's not, and that's what hurts the most. I'm not little like Xander. I can handle the truth.

I jerk open the fridge door a little too hard and the pickle jars clink together. When I go to pull out the drawer for the veggies, it comes right off in my hand. It takes three tries to get it back into place.

"Drew." Mom turns around to face me. "That's enough."

I toss a bag of spinach onto the kitchen table. It slides across and then falls to the floor.

Mom eyeballs me, but she doesn't say anything more about it. Sometimes silence is the worst. "Can you finish making dinner while I tidy up a bit?"

So maybe she didn't know he was coming *tonight*. Maybe she's not lying about that part.

"I'd really appreciate it. You've been doing such a good job with that artichoke sauce. And we have a few cans in the pantry." Her eyes linger on me, pleading.

"Fine," I mumble.

She mouths "thank you" and snatches the laundry basket from the dining room before heading up the stairs.

I heat up some olive oil in a pan and start chopping onions and garlic. Once I have those sizzling on the stove top, I set four place mats on the table, and grab the cans of artichoke hearts and peeled tomatoes from the pantry. Is there any smell better than garlic in olive oil? Well, maybe warm chocolate chip cookies. Still, the smell of the sauce coming together calms me down a notch.

I'm chopping up the artichoke hearts on the cutting board when Xander pads into the room behind me.

"Is Filipe coming for dinner?" he asks.

I wish. "No."

"Then why are there four place mats?"

"Mom's *friend* is coming."

"Ashley?"

"No."

"Mrs. Eisenberg?"

"No."

"Is it—"

"Stop, Xan."

"Why are you so grouchy?"

"It's Mom's friend from out of town. Phil."

"A friend's visiting? Cool."

Xander pads back into the living room to watch his show, and I chop harder.

HE'S LATE.

The pasta's been done for a good fifteen minutes, but the sauce still simmers on the stove. As I stirred and stirred it, I added more and more red pepper flakes. Mom, Xander, and I can stand the heat, but can he?

While the pasta sits in the strainer by the sink getting all stuck together, Mom keeps checking her phone. I swear she's redone her ponytail about fifty trillion times.

Xan and I sit at the kitchen table. He's looking

about ready to eat his napkin when the doorbell rings. While Mom's answering the door, I switch over to Dad's old spot. "You don't sit there," Xan says.

"I do tonight." I hope the glare I shoot him tells him to leave it be, at least until that guy leaves.

We can't see the front door from the kitchen, which is fine by me. I don't want to know what Mom does when she sees this guy. Do they hug? Does he kiss her? Does she kiss him? I swallow hard at the thought. I want to be able to eat my dinner without barfing it up.

He and Mom walk into the kitchen. Mom's hair is down now. Down, up. Down, up. If she can't decide how she wants her hair, maybe she isn't so certain he'll be staying with us after all, right? *A couple days.*

"Xan, Drew, I'd like you to meet my friend Phil. Phil and I went to high school together. Gosh, that's a lot longer ago than it feels, huh?"

"What's your last name?" Xan asks. Ever since the spring, he's been obsessed with everyone's last names and learning how to spell them.

Mom gives Xan a *be on your best behavior or else* eyeball.

"Pittman," he says.

"Okay, so . . . um, P. I. T. . . ."

"Honey, he can show you how to spell it later," Mom says. "After dinner." She turns to Phil. "Well, these are my boys. Drew's twelve and Xander is six."

"And a quarter." Xan nods for emphasis.

Mom licks her lips. "Well, um, how about you have a seat, Phil. I'll just serve up this pasta and, um, get you a glass of—is water all right?"

Whenever Mom has a difficult patron at the library, she describes every single thing she's doing out loud. Maybe it makes her less nervous. Or maybe it makes her feel like she's in control instead of the cranky, pushy person. Why's she doing it with Phil, though? If he's *just an old friend* like she said, what reason would she have to be so nervous?

Now that I'm in Dad's seat, Phil is directly across from me. I didn't think this out so well.

Mom sets down plates of spaghetti in front of Xan and me. When she comes back with plates for her and Phil, I notice that her eyelashes look longer and darker. Did she put on makeup for him?

She sits in her usual seat and places her napkin on her lap. "I can't remember," she says to Phil. "Do you—did your folks say grace?"

Phil shakes his head. "We were lucky if the food made it to the table before it got gobbled up." He laughs.

Mom laughs too. Even though it's not like what he said was that funny.

"Well," Mom says, blushing. "Let's dig in."

PHIL'S BARELY POPPED IN A BITE OF

pasta when he starts to cough. "Whew," he says, reaching for his glass of water, "that's got some kick, Kayla."

Mom side-eyes me.

"What?" I mouth.

Xan pushes his pasta to the back corner of his plate.

I swirl a big honking bite around my fork and shove the whole thing in my mouth. Oh man. Maybe I did go a little overboard with the red pepper flakes. My tongue tingles and burns something fierce. But I can't let Phil see. No way. Thankfully, I know the secret trick. The thing I have that Phil doesn't: milk.

I reach for my glass and take a long drink, calming the fire in my throat. "Doesn't seem too hot to me," I say with a shrug.

"Drew's been such a big help around the house ever since . . ." Mom clears her throat.

"My dad died," Xander blurts out.

I reach my foot under the table and give my brother a little kick. Why does this dude need to know?

"I'm so sorry, bud. It's really hard to lose someone you love." Phil glances over at Mom after he says it. But the weirder part is the way he sounds. Like it's not actually news to him. Like he's prepared, maybe even practiced for this moment.

"Yeah," Xan says quietly. "Except I don't really remember him so much." He shrugs and takes a cautiously small bite of spaghetti.

Phil reaches across the table and gently pats his hand.

I tuck my left hand under my leg in case that kind of behavior is contagious.

"Drew's gotten really into cooking," Mom says. "Though maybe he took it a little too far with the spice rack tonight."

"I know my way around a kitchen pretty well, myself. So, Drew, is spaghetti your specialty?"

There's something about the way he says it. The tiniest bit of sarcasm, but not enough that Mom seems to pick up on it.

"Yeah. I make a real mean boxed mac and cheese. And you should see the toast I made the other day."

"Drew!" Mom gives me the eye. "Cut it out."

"What?"

"You know what? I'm sorry, Drew. I wasn't trying to offend you at all. It's just—I'm into cooking too, and I can appreciate the effort here. It would be nice to talk recipes with you sometime. Hear some of your favorites. Us guys who know our way around the kitchen, we need to stick together, right?" He swirls his fork around in the spaghetti. As he puts it in his mouth, a bit of the sauce sticks to the bottom of his lip. Mom dabs at her mouth to tell him.

I slurp up another forkful so I can get away without saying anything back.

Us guys who know our way around the kitchen? Guys?

How about nine years old with a brother still in diapers and a mom who could barely get out of bed. Grandma had gone back home to California, con-

vinced we were doing better. The truth is, we did eat mac and cheese. But not even the boxed kind yet—the microwave kind from Trader Joe's. And toast, burned half the time.

That was the best I could do.

I try to swallow away that ball in my throat, the one that comes back every now and then. My eyes smart. Guess maybe the sauce was too spicy, even for me.

The first time I tried to make rice and it all burned and stuck to the pot. That time I didn't know the difference between a bulb of garlic and a clove. It's like a highlight reel playing in my head, except actually more like a low-light reel. When I finally pull myself out of it, Mom and Phil are catching up on the life history of every single person they know from high school. Next comes Phil's interrogation of Xan and me. Questions like: What's your favorite sport? (Me: Um. Xan: Tennis.) And: What do you want to be when you grow up? (Me: A lawyer or an architect. Xan: A blacksmith.) Mom says she still isn't sure what she wants to be when she grows up, and I catch him smiling at her in this dumb, goofy way like they're in a romantic comedy.

I don't think I can take it for one second longer.

"Can I be excused?" I ask Mom.

"Me too? I'm done," Xander says, even though he's only eaten half the food on his plate.

Mom glances at Phil, as if there's something the two of them have to decide.

"Sure, boys," she says, but her eyes aren't looking at either of us.

I grab my plate and Xan's and bring them to the sink. Mom looks like she wants to keep sitting there, talking to Phil all night. *Old friend?* Sure, Mom. Sure. Filipe was right.

"Leave the dishes, Drew," Mom says. "I'll take care of them later."

I put my glass down on top of the plates with a clink.

"Can you help get your brother ready for bed?"

I look at the clock. "It's only seven thirty. And it's summer."

"He seems tired. And there's something going around at his camp. Honey, please?"

Xan's already dumped out a box of Legos in the living room.

"Mom says you've got to get ready for bed," I tell him.

"Already?"

Someone wants some alone time. With Phil. The thought makes my stomach clench again.

I lower my voice. "You can still play upstairs in your room. Just . . . quieter."

"Okay," Xan says.

As he puts on his pajamas and brushes his teeth, I lean against the wall in the upstairs hallway, wondering what he thinks about Phil. How does his six-and-a-quarter-year-old brain make sense of this guy we never heard of before just appearing at our door? Helping himself to our food. Sitting at our table with us. Looking at Mom like that.

The thing is, we *know* Mom's friends. Mom's friends don't look anything like him. For one, they shower regularly. And two, they do not drive around on motorcycles. They drive cars like normal people.

Xan lets out a big yawn. So maybe Mom's right. Maybe he really is sleepy.

"You sure you want to play?"

Xan climbs into his bed. "Read me a story?"

I grab *Dory Fantasmagory* from his bookshelf and start reading. A few pages in, Xan closes his eyes, and then his breathing slows way down and I know he's asleep.

Downstairs Mom and Phil are still talking in the kitchen, the dirty dishes piled in the sink. Part of me wants to start cleaning up and see if all that noise makes a difference, but the other part of me worries they won't even notice. I slip out the sliding glass door.

It's dark outside and quiet, except for the crickets and the frogs. As I step off the deck and down into the grass, the outside light comes on, lighting up the whole backyard. If they're paying attention, maybe they'll wonder who's out here. Maybe they'll think it's a burglar or something.

But they aren't going to notice, are they?

I pad through the grass and into the shed, which until a few weeks ago was covered in cobwebs and overgrown vines. I close the door behind me and flick on the light. After a few minutes, that outside light will go off—it's motion sensitive. They won't know I'm out here. The shed doesn't have any windows facing the house, only a skylight and a big window looking out the back of it where Dad set up bird feeders.

Inside, it's a mess. One of Mom's friends at the library—Julia—convinced her it was time to do something with this place. Turn it into a "she shed." I know, right? I guess it's a thing now. Right now it's still in transition. Boxes everywhere. Cans of paint that Mom still hasn't opened. What kind of color even is *perfect greige*, anyway? Dad's old Paw Sox pennant from before they moved to Worcester sticks out of one of the boxes—there are so many of them. One whole stack, box after box labeled FRAGILE.

Fragile. Why didn't someone bother to label Dad like that? Maybe then I would've known what could happen. Maybe then it wouldn't have been such a shock.

The thing no one tells you when you get older is how the stuff you believed so easily when you were nine doesn't make sense anymore. Not just Santa and the tooth fairy, but the big stuff. Like when you get called out of class one Tuesday and your mom is there in the front office with her best friend and her eyes are puffy and her cardigan is falling off her shoulders but she doesn't even seem to notice. And then, when you finally get back home after a car ride that seems to last a lifetime even though there's only ten minutes, tops, between school and home, she says words that don't make any sense at all. That your dad—your *Dad*—killed himself.

Other people, you learn, other people will use

the words "committed suicide," but that's not true. He didn't choose it. His brain was sick—those were the exact words Mom used—and he couldn't see that there were other choices. That there was help. I knew what it was like to get sick. Nobody *chooses* to get sick.

But three years is a long time. And now I don't know. If Dad was so sick, if he really was depressed, how come I couldn't tell? He was my *dad*. I should have been able to tell that something was wrong. And if I hadn't been able to tell that something was wrong with him, that meant that other people, other people I knew, could be in pain, could be sick the way my dad was.

And if there were other options, how come he couldn't see them? He was smart, my dad. The smartest person I knew.

It was easy to believe it then, the things Mom and the counselor said to me. They were adults, and I was only nine. They knew more than me then. But the more I thought about it, the more I turned it over in my mind the past few years, all of it just fell apart. I kept looking for clues, remembering the days leading up to when it happened. But I couldn't come up with anything. Not one thing.

For a few months after Dad died, on Wednesday

evenings Mom would take me to Chad's House. It was a big yellow Victorian up on a hill in Providence where I'd hang out with all these other kids who had someone they loved die from suicide. We were members of the worst club ever. They were the only people I've ever met who "got" it—who understood that it was different, how Dad died.

When I went back to school after, my third-grade teacher, Mrs. Sprouse, kept trying to make me feel okay talking about it. She'd let me know if another kid in my class lost their grandpa or their pet. As if it was *at all* the same thing.

But even the kids at Chad's House, none of them entirely understood what it was like for me. Trina's dad had been in trouble with drugs before, so Trina had to live with her grandparents. And Liam's mom had been depressed for a long time, had actually tried to kill herself before. All of them had known for years that things weren't okay with their parents. It didn't happen out of nowhere, not like with my dad.

The only way I could make sense of it was by believing—accepting, or trying to, anyway—that my dad was a liar. He had lied about everything. For years—my whole life—he had pretended to be happy when clearly he wasn't. He'd tricked us all into believing nothing was wrong when actually something was very, very wrong.

He'd faked his whole life with us. And it was a nice life, too, with the four of us. He and Mom didn't fight, not like some parents. The weekend before he died, we went on this big camping trip with Filipe's family. And Dad seemed totally normal. He definitely wasn't sad. He had three s'mores that last night. Three. I mean, who does that and then kills themself?

Maybe if he'd just told the truth, he would still be here. With me—with us.

I step over the paint cans and pull out one of the boxes labeled FRAGILE. The top is dusty, like these boxes have been packed up for a while. I never came in here to see. I didn't want to see Dad's stuff—Dad's life—in boxes. I slip off the top and reach my hand through all the foam peanuts until I touch glass.

I know what it is before I even lift out the clear glass bottle and peer at the ship inside. For how small it is, there's so much detail.

Dad used to spend hours in here, long into the night sometimes. Painting these ships, with parts so tiny he had to use a magnifying glass. He'd have a ball game playing on the radio, or sometimes music.

So many hours in here, all by himself. He couldn't just read a book while Xan and I watched TV or played, like Filipe's dad. He had to hide away in a shed in his own backyard.

Fragile.

I shake the bottle, at first just a little shake. All those tiny, perfect pieces of wood that he spent hours painting and collapsing and then lifting up inside. Tinier than toothpicks, a sail rigged between them just so. His perfect ship in that perfect bottle in that perfect shed of his. What a lie.

I shake it harder, hard, hard, hardest until the wood splinters and cracks, wood hitting wood hitting glass. And when I'm done, the only thing left intact is the bottle.

For a minute I stand there, just holding it, my heart still beating rapidly in my chest as I stare at what I did. The kind of thing I would've gotten in big trouble for back when I was little. Sent to my room. Or worse, forced to have a never-ending conversation with Mom at the kitchen table about *why* I had done it and what I was feeling. Back when Mom was the parent and I was the kid.

But as far as I know, Mom doesn't even look in these boxes. No one will ever know except me, and that feels right.

I carefully place the bottle back where I found it, mixed in with all the foam peanuts, and place the top back on the box.

If only I could just put all of my feelings about Dad into a box, close it up, and leave them in here forever. If only.

WHEN I STEP OUT INTO THE BACKYARD,

something has changed. All the lights are on now in my house. Even upstairs.

I walk across the yard and slide open the glass door. Mom has her cell phone pressed to her ear and she whips around at the screech of the door. Phil sits on the sofa, flipping through a magazine.

"So sorry to bother you, Adriana, he's right here, I—I know. Thanks." Mom sets her phone down on the mantel, her brow furrowing as she looks at me. "Where were you?"

I hold my hand limply by my side, imagining that ship how it was when I saw it, and then how I left it. A million tiny broken pieces. "Just outside." I gesture to the shed.

Mom runs her hand through her hair. "You haven't been in the shed in years! I never—I couldn't find you. I called your cell phone. I thought maybe you went over to Filipe's. Drew, I was—"

From the couch, Phil stares at me as if I did something terribly wrong to upset my mom.

"All I did was go outside. It's my own backyard." That ball in my throat is back, growing larger by the second as my eyes shift from Mom to Phil, Phil to Mom. What else am I supposed to say?

"Can I go to my room now?" The voice that comes out of my throat sounds small. Weak. Like it's me trapped in the bottom of a boat inside a bottle.

Mom nods, but as I head upstairs, I can hear their voices. Mom's is quiet; Phil's a little too loud. She's still upset, but he's calming her down. Or trying to. It doesn't make any sense. I didn't even go anywhere. I mean, why would she think something bad happened? The whole time I was a hundred feet away. All she had to do was look for me. But no, to really do that, she would have to stop thinking about Phil for five seconds.

Back in my bedroom, my cell phone is plugged into the charger. When I pick it up, I see the missed calls that came in while I was outside. Five of them, all from Mom. And the texts: Where are you? Please call me.

I hate that I made her worry about me. One by one I swipe to delete the messages. I've just deleted the last one when my phone buzzes with a brand-new text from Filipe. Dude, where'd you go? Your mom was freaking out.

Outside in the shed, I type. She didn't look there.

What's even in there?

All that's left of my dad. Except I can't type that. I can't say stuff like that to Filipe. He'd never get it. His dad is normal. His dad is alive.

Just some old stuff. I was bored. NBD.

Are you in trouble?

IDK.

There's a knock on my door.

Hold on, I text him, then silence my phone and slide it under the unmade covers of my bed. I clear my throat. "Yeah?"

My mom opens the door. "Can we talk for a few minutes, hon?"

I shrug.

She closes the door behind her and sits down on my bed by the pillow. "You're not in trouble," Mom says, her voice calmer now. "In case you were wondering."

"Okay."

"It was foolish of me not to think to look outside. But it was so quiet after you put Xan to bed, and when I checked in your room, Drew, you were gone, and I . . . I panicked."

"You're just mad I made you look bad in front of Phil."

Mom looks taken aback. "Hon, that's not it at all."

What is it, then? But I don't ask. Honestly, I just want to go to bed. Pretend this whole night didn't happen, wake up, and find Phil's motorcycle gone. He's on a bike trip? Cool. Maybe he needs to hit the road a little early. Buh-bye. See ya.

Mom folds down the top of my sheet, tidying my bed. It's pointless. I'm about to go to sleep in it anyway. "You know, we need to talk about things like we promised. Not let them fester until they're so big we don't think we can handle them."

She waits for me to say something back. But there's nothing to say. She's the one who didn't communicate something. She's the one who kept a secret. So maybe it isn't as big as those secrets Dad kept, but it's a secret all the same. She knew Phil was coming. She knew and she didn't tell me.

"Drew." Mom grabs for my hand like I'm some little kid. I jerk it back. "Tell me what's going through your head. I'm here for you."

"Trust me, you don't want to hear it." I sit on my hands.

"That's not true."

I suck in a deep breath. Once I start, I might not be able to stop. It'll all come flooding out of me, fire-hydrant style. But she's still waiting, so I let loose. "Phil Pittman, Mom? Is that even his real name? I mean, what kind of name is that? And what the heck is he doing here? How long did you know he was going to come? You could've said something to Xan and me like with those other dates. How come you didn't? That's messed up, you know?"

My heart thunders in my chest as I stare back at Mom.

You didn't really *want to know all of that, did you?*

Mom reaches a hand back, playing with my sheet again. "Well, that was honest, at least. You're right, though. I'm sorry things didn't go according to plan this time. I always intended to tell you and your brother about Phil's visit in advance. What can I say? He came two weeks earlier than he was supposed to, catching everyone—all of us, me included—by surprise. You know, I probably would've cleaned up the house a little if I'd known he was coming today." She laughs for a second, her eyes pleading with me.

I want to be able to buy it. But all I can hear is what Filipe said. And I don't have enough to prove him wrong. Not yet. Especially with the way Phil kept looking at Mom during dinner. Never mind how Mom looked at him.

"Is there anything else?" Mom twists her wedding ring and suddenly my heart slows down. It's still there. What does that mean? If she was really interested in Phil, she'd take it off, right? When your husband dies, you don't have to keep wearing the ring forever. "I'm happy to tell you a little more about how this all came together, if that would help."

I shrug. "Fine."

"A few months ago, Phil and I connected on

• 58 •

Facebook. We sent a few messages back and forth. You know, just two old friends finding each other. Happens all the time these days with social media. I told him he was welcome to stay with us for a few days when he made it out to Rhode Island. That was supposed to be the week after the Fourth of July, but when Steve from our class broke his leg on a hike out in Western Mass, Phil decided to swing through Rhode Island ahead of schedule."

"So where's he from?"

"Phil or Steve?"

I don't care about some mutual friend named Steve. "Phil."

"He's kind of between places right now."

"He's *homeless*? Does he even have a job?"

"Andrew James McCormack." Mom's voice turns stern. "I didn't raise you to speak like this. That's not how we treat . . . anyone." She stares back at me like she doesn't even recognize her own son. I know the feeling.

I wish I'd just gone over to Filipe's instead of the shed. Then maybe I could've spent the night. Been anywhere but here.

Mom glances at the clock on my nightstand. "It's

getting late and I need to set up the guest bedroom for Phil." She stands up, still watching me. That look of shock lingers on her face. Like she can't believe I'd have the nerve to say that stuff about Phil.

She doesn't correct any of the things I said, though, so maybe I wasn't wrong.

She pauses by my door, like maybe she wants to say something else, but then she tucks a piece of hair behind her ear and closes her mouth. "Good night."

"Night," I mutter.

She closes the door tight behind her, and finally I'm alone.

A stack of books from the library sits on my bedside table—the new Rick Riordan, this nonfiction book about spies, and a couple novels from the seventh-grade summer reading list. I flip through them for a few minutes, but nothing holds my attention.

And then out of nowhere it hits me, why Mom was so panicked when she couldn't find me.

Does she worry I'm like Dad? Or that I could be someday? That I'd turn into him?

There are so many things I still wonder, but I'm afraid to ask. Never mind; who do you even ask a question like that to? Not Filipe, that's for sure. And not Mom. It would only freak her out. Especially if she's already worried about it.

Do you wake up one day wanting to kill yourself? Or is it something you think about for a while first? For days, weeks, months. Years?

Both sound so awful, I don't know which is worse. Or which was true for Dad.

I wish she'd just told me that was why she was so worried. Because then I could have told her without freaking her out that, no, I'm not like that at all. I would never. Could never.

Except—what if it was in Dad's DNA, what he did? Did he pass it along to me?

I bolt out of bed, shivering at the thought. No one's in the bathroom across the hall, so I use this chance to wash up. I brush my teeth forever, wishing that fear away, but it's like it's lodged in my brain now.

When I climb back into bed, I open up the Rick Riordan. His books always take me on an adventure somewhere else, far away from my problems. This one's no different, and before I know it, I'm on page fifty, barely able to keep my eyes open. I slip in my bookmark and shut off the light.

As I'm starting to doze off, I hear Mom's footsteps

on the stairs, accompanied by heavier ones. "Now's not the time to tell him," she says. "He's not ready yet."

Tell who what? Ready for . . . what?

Does she mean me?

But I can barely hold the question in my mind for more than a few seconds before I drift off to sleep.

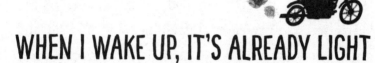

WHEN I WAKE UP, IT'S ALREADY LIGHT

out. Five thirty is way, way too early to get up, so I roll onto my other side, shut my eyes, and try to push back the memories of everything that happened last night.

Easier said than done.

Just as I'm starting to fall back to sleep, I hear a noise like the sound of two friends high-fiving each other. Again. Again. And again. *What the heck?* Eyes open, I listen harder. "Six. Seven. Eight." The counting is coming from our backyard.

I tiptoe over to the window and then quickly pull

my head to the side and out of sight. Facing my window, doing jumping jacks in his pajama pants and a T-shirt, is Phil.

"Thirty-two. Thirty-three. Thirty-four."

What. A. Weirdo.

I peek again, this time for longer. Phil stares straight ahead, not up at the second floor where I am. I scan the yard. As far as I can tell, Mom isn't out there and neither is Xander.

What kind of person does jumping jacks at five thirty in the morning?

When I get back into bed, I can still hear him. "Fifty-seven. Fifty-eight. Fifty-nine." On and on and on. What does he think our house is, some kind of army boot camp? The rest of us are trying to sleep, you know?

Finally I press both hands to my ears. Even though it sounds like the ocean, at least I don't have to listen to him.

I wake up again to the sound of the bathroom shower and, from the living room, Xander's cartoons. I toss on some clean clothes and make my way down the stairs.

It smells like bacon and pancakes and coffee. My stomach rumbles. Mom never cooks breakfast on weekdays unless it's one of our birthdays—she's too busy running around to get us all out the door in time.

I round the corner into the kitchen. Phil's got his back to me as he whisks a bowl next to the stove. Xan is sitting at the counter, dunking pancakes in syrup.

"Looks like somebody's up and at 'em," Phil says as he transfers some bacon to a plate covered with paper towels.

"His name's not Adam, it's Drew!" Xander giggles.

"You want chocolate chips or blueberries in your pancakes?"

I reach in the cupboard for some cereal. "No thanks."

"Not much of a breakfast person?"

I shake the box of granola. There's barely any left.

"Not much of a morning person?"

"Looks like you are," I mutter, thinking back to earlier this morning.

"You got me." He tosses some frozen blueberries into the half-cooked pancakes on the stove. "Always been a morning person."

I scoot out of Phil's way in search of some milk for my granola.

"Sorry for taking over your kitchen," Phil says. "Thought your mom might appreciate a morning off kitchen duty."

I clink a spoon into my bowl. *A morning off?* Does he think I never help out around here? That it isn't me getting Xan his breakfast most mornings while Mom's upstairs blow-drying her hair and getting dressed for work?

"I hear you're heading off to the library with your mom soon. You both bring a lunch? Anything I can make?"

I leave my granola behind and hop over to the fridge before he can try to take over this, too. "I'm twelve," I say. "I've been making my own lunch for years."

Phil raises both hands up in the air like he's been caught red-handed and Xan laughs like Phil's hilarious. *Traitor.* Phil knows how to get my brother on his side: right through his stomach. He'll have to work a lot harder with me.

I finish slapping together a PB and J and take my soggy granola into the living room, where I turn up the TV volume as high as I can get away with and sling my feet over the side of the sofa.

Right after my dad died, my grandma flew out from California to stay with us. The morning before her flight back to California, three days after the funeral, Grandma pulled me aside. She bent her knees so she was at my height. Her breath smelled like ciga-rettes covered up with cinnamon chewing gum.

"You've got to help your mother around the house now that your father, well . . ." Like everyone else, she had trouble saying the words. Either she didn't want to or she didn't know how. "You're the man of the house now, Drew. But you can handle it. You've always been a responsible little boy. You keep an eye on your mother, you hear?"

I heard. Loud and clear.

"Okay, Grandma."

She smiled and eased herself back up to standing and called for a cab to take her to the airport.

I was nine. She was a grown-up. So I took her at her word. It was my job, mine, to keep everything together. No one was going to swoop in and save us. It was on me.

Who does Phil think he is, anyway? Coming in here, trying to take over everything. Someone does something like that, it makes you wonder. The guy's got to have some kind of ulterior motive, right?

Xander's too little to think twice about it, but not me. No, Phil's got an agenda, secret or not, and I'm going to get to the bottom of it.

LATER THAT MORNING AT THE LIBRARY,

I've just finished helping the last kid from morning story hour pick out his summer reading prize when I hear a whimper come from the nonfiction section.

"Audrey, did you hear that?"

Audrey whips around in her rolling chair at the computer, where Mrs. Eisenberg left her to look at websites for different STEM projects. "Hear what?"

I strain my ears. Sniffles, I'm sure of it.

"Can you hand out some prizes if anyone needs help?"

Until Mrs. Eisenberg comes back from her meeting upstairs, Audrey and I are in charge. As much as Audrey will let *me* be in charge of anything. Okay, I'll be honest, it pretty much means Audrey's in charge.

I get up from behind Mrs. Eisenberg's desk, where she keeps the summer reading prizes, and walk over to the nonfiction section.

A little boy, maybe three years old, sits with his back against the shelves that hold the fairy-tale books. Tears stream down his round, red cheeks.

"Hey there." I crouch down and use my quiet voice. "It's okay, buddy. Who'd you come here with?"

He gulps back some tears. "I want my mommy."

"Did you come here with her?"

He stares back at me, his face blank.

"Who did you come here with?" I stand up for a second and wave at Audrey. "Can you give me a hand?"

I squat back down next to him. "We're going to get in touch with your mom or dad or babysitter. Don't worry. What's your name?"

He rubs his eyes with a chubby little fist. "Benny."

"Okay, Benny. I'm Drew." Audrey comes to a stop right next to me. "And this is Audrey."

"Why's he crying?" she asks.

"Why do you think, Audrey? He's lost."

"Oh," she says. "Oh no. Someone left him here? Who leaves a little kid at the library all by themselves?" Her eyes look strangely panicked. Get it together, Audrey. He's a three-year-old, not a grizzly bear.

"Audrey." My voice gets sharp. "You're not helping."

I reach my hand out for Benny's. "Come with me. We're going to go use the intercom! Doesn't that sound fun?"

"But Mrs. Eisenberg said . . ."

"She's not here right now," I snap at Audrey. "*We're* in charge." Actually, that's wrong. If someone is taking charge right now, it's me.

Benny clutches my hand as we walk back over to Mrs. Eisenberg's desk, where her big black phone sits next to stacks of catalogs and magazines. The thing's got at least a dozen buttons and doubles as an intercom. Sure, Mrs. Eisenberg showed me how to use it last summer, but we haven't had any emergencies since then and I barely remember how it works. Still. One look at Benny's trembling lower lip tells me some things are worth doing, even if you might make a mistake.

I lift up the receiver and push the intercom button. "Hello? Is this thing on?" I can't hear anything. *Hmm.* I try again, pushing the intercom button, and then pick up the receiver. "Hello?" This time, my voice blares out from the phone's speaker. That must mean it's blaring out of the speakers on all the phones upstairs.

"If you came to the library with Benny, he's still down in the children's room. Um . . ." What am I supposed to say next? We never practiced this part, and we haven't had any lost kids here before. But I heard them do it at the grocery store once.

"Again, that's Benny. He's, I think, three? And he's down in the children's room with, uh, me, Drew." Audrey glares at me. Do I have to include her too? Oh, fine. "And Audrey," I add.

It's only when I hang up the phone that I can feel my heart pounding in my ears.

"What if nobody comes?" Audrey says. Clearly she's seen too many stories on the news about kids getting abandoned. His mom or dad is probably somewhere in the library. One of those parents who think the librarian's a free babysitter. Still, I know I'll feel better once Benny's back in their arms.

"I'm sure someone's going to come right away." I

glance at Benny, whose eyes still look big and worried.

"I have an idea!" I say in my puppet performer voice—all confidence and smiles. Fake it till you make it, right? "Hey, Benny, would you want to choose something from this box to play with while we wait?" I pull out one of the prize boxes and place it in front of Benny.

As he picks through the various cheap plastic dinosaurs and rubber balls, I tell him some of the dinosaur names—well, the ones I remember. I was never as into dinos as Xan. There's a short, fat blue-green one that I call *Stumpyosaurus*. The name gets a laugh out of Benny. So does the little dance I have him do.

A few minutes later, the elevator door bursts open. "Benny!" A woman with frizzy blond hair in a ponytail pushes a double-wide stroller with two crying babies.

"I'm so, so, so sorry. Oh, Benny." She swoops in and picks him up, hugging him close to her chest. To me she says, "I don't know where my mind is today. I could've sworn he was with the sitter, but he wasn't, he was here with me and the twins—try telling that to my sleep-deprived brain. Oh, you're a savior. What's your name again?"

"Drew."

Benny holds up the Stumpyosaurus. "Mommy, can I keep him?"

I flash his mom a thumbs-up.

"Are you sure?" Benny's mom looks back at me.

"Yeah, of course."

"Thank you." She squeezes Benny again. "Oh, honey, I'm so sorry about that. Mommy would never forget about you." She pushes the stroller back and forth, not that it seems to matter for the screaming twins. At least one of them is totally overdue for a diaper change.

"Well, we should probably get out of here before we make an even bigger scene. Thanks again for saving the day. Another minute and I would've been in my car heading home."

After she leaves, the children's room goes quiet, empty in the way it only is on slow summer mornings after story hour. Anyone who has a choice is at the beach or in the park tossing a Frisbee.

Audrey makes her way back to the computer.

Clickety-clack-click.

I cross my arms behind my head and spin around in Mrs. Eisenberg's chair.

"Hey, Drew?"

I stick out my leg to catch the edge of the desk and come to a stop.

"Yeah?"

"You were really good," she says. "With Benny."

Am I dizzy from the spinning or did Audrey actually just admit that *I* was good at something?

"I didn't know what to do, but you did."

She's right. "Wait," I say, as suddenly it all falls into place. "Are you . . . afraid of *kids*?"

Audrey shifts her gaze to the carpet. "Kind of."

It all makes sense now, how she acted yesterday. The children's room has to be about the last place she'd want to be stuck for the entire summer. No wonder she wants to show Mrs. Eisenberg how good she is with computers—anything to get away from the rug rats. She's not trying to replace or one-up me at all.

"But honestly, Drew. *Stumpyosaurus*?"

Audrey smiles, and I return to spinning.

9

MAYBE AUDREY ISN'T GOING TO BE

the actual worst for the whole summer. For the rest of the day at the library, she's actually okay. I mean, it's not like we're suddenly best friends or anything. Between Benny getting left behind and everything else, I almost forget what's waiting for me back at home. Almost.

"From what Mrs. Eisenberg told me, it sounds like you and Audrey are starting to get along," Mom says as we pull out of the parking spot at the library and head down the road to pick up Xan.

"I guess," I say. "She's all right."

"I didn't know if you'd take to sharing your turf with someone."

"My turf?"

"You know . . . It's kind of your terrain down there. Sometimes it's hard to have someone come along and start changing things up."

I shrug.

Mom leaves me in the car with the AC running while she goes into the Y to fetch my brother. I keep thinking about what she said as the voices on the radio debate the Providence mayor's latest budget proposal. The person who's trying to take over my turf—it's not Audrey at all. It's Phil.

At least I only have to put up with him for a few days, though. Soon he'll be zooming off on his motorcycle, never to be heard from again, right? I suck in a deep breath. Just a few days. How many is a few, anyway? Two? Nah, that's a couple. Three, then? Four, tops. And we've already survived one.

Next thing I know, Xander's sliding into the back seat and telling us all about his day at camp and how fast he's getting at swimming and how this one kid peed in the pool when no one was looking, and before long we're turning down our street. I brace myself for the motorcycle in our driveway, suddenly wondering what in the heck Phil did all day.

And then there he is. Pushing the mower through our yard. My jaw tightens.

"I was going to do that tonight," I say to Mom as we pull into the driveway. Up close now, I spot the chest hair sticking out of the top of Phil's shirt, and the pit stains under his arms. *Gross.*

"Aw, Drew. He was around and he offered. This way you have more time to hang out with Filipe, be a kid for once."

As I step out of the car, I search for evidence that he somehow messed the whole thing up. Maybe he didn't get the edges right around the walkway. Or his lines are uneven. But I can't find anything wrong with it.

Maybe he didn't get to the backyard yet! Maybe I can still do that, at least. I race around the house. But when I get there, all I see are the clean, straight lines left by the mower. Something else is different too.

Not the deck. Not the back of the house. Not the shed. It's the shrubs. All the stuff that's grown wild over the past three years. I thought Mom liked it that way. Or that she didn't care. But he's gone to town, hacking it to pieces. *I* could've done that.

Why's he helping around the house so much, anyway? Suddenly it hits me, a truth I hadn't considered. What if Mom wasn't lying last night when she said Phil *was* an old friend?

Maybe that's all he was back then. She never talked about who her boyfriends were back in high school—not that I'd asked—and she didn't meet my dad until grad school. Anyway. Maybe she just can't see what's so obvious now: that Phil had—*has*—a crush on her.

Somehow he found out about Dad and now he's making his move.

Man, what didn't he do while we were at the library all day? I'm almost afraid to go inside the house and find out. I head into the living room, and even from there the smells from the kitchen are overpowering. Curry and cumin and chicken. I curse my mouth for watering at whatever it is he's been making. I spot the slow cooker on the counter. Everything I tried to make in that thing always ended up a pile of mush, so I gave up on it.

The door into the garage creaks open and Mom steps in. "Wow," she says. "Smells pretty tasty in here."

Xander races in under her arm, slipping out of his sneakers and darting toward the living room.

"One hour of screen time," Mom reminds him. She fills up a glass of water and brings it to the door. Sweat dripping off his forehead, Phil looms in the doorframe and takes the glass of water from Mom.

"I'm going to head upstairs to change out of my work clothes," Mom says. "I'll be right back."

She disappears up the stairs, leaving me alone with Phil.

"So." Phil sets his empty glass on the counter. "How was the library today? Did you read lots of books?"

I roll my eyes. "You don't *read books* when you *work* there."

Phil laughs. "I didn't realize you were working already. Aren't there laws about child labor? I thought you had to be at least fifteen or sixteen to work."

"I don't *technically* work there. Not yet . . ." It's hard to explain without somehow making it sound like babysitting. Which it *is not*. "Anyway. I don't get to read. Even the librarian doesn't sit around reading books. We're really busy."

"Cool, cool. You know, I've had the chance to visit so many different libraries all over the country the past few months. It's pretty amazing how unique they are. And some of the facilities—you should see some of the cool new buildings the architects are coming up with. You mentioned you wanted to be an architect someday, right?"

What does he want? For me to give him bonus points because he remembered me saying that last night? I shrug. "When are you going back out again on your bike?"

"Pretty soon. It's nice to have a few days off the road. That much riding really wears on your body, you know?"

As if I know one thing about motorcycles. "Not really," I say.

"Anyway, in the meantime, I thought your mom might appreciate having some extra help around here."

She might have, I think, when we needed it. Three years ago. I stare up at him, my mouth still zippered shut. I want to tell him I'm onto him, but I can't get the words out as he dorkily stares back at me.

There's nothing left for either of us to say to each other. No more small talk to make, anyway.

I chew on the inside of my cheek, searching for an out. "I'm going over to my friend's house," I say, heading for the door behind him. "Across the street."

"Don't you think you should check with your mom first?"

Who does he think he is, my dad?

He leaves just enough room for me to squeeze by him and out the door, all without saying another word.

OUT IN THE YARD AND AWAY FROM

Phil, I can finally breathe again.

Check with my mom first?

Filipe's is practically my second home, dude. Maybe you should check with your *mom. Last I heard, it wasn't exactly safe to ride motorcycles.*

As I cross the street, I hear the *bop, bop, bop* of the basketball bouncing on the pavement. Nothing sounds so good right now as watching a shot swish through the net.

"Hey!" I yell, but as I get closer, I can see Filipe's

not out there by himself. And he's not with Anibal either. Theo, one of the eighth graders from the soccer team, is sipping a lime Gatorade. He sets it down on the pavement just in time to receive a pass from Filipe and take a three-pointer. The kind I only make about once a century.

The ball swooshes through the net.

"Nice one," Filipe says before saying anything back to me.

"Hey, Drew." Theo jogs to the hoop. He bounces the ball, switching from his left hand to his right. He makes it look easy. Let's face it: Theo makes every sport look easy. He's pretty much the best athlete in the eighth grade—well, except for Chloe Ramer, who's nationally ranked in tennis.

"Think fast!"

He chucks the ball straight at me and I barely have time to get my hands out for it. It smacks off my elbow, bouncing down the pavement toward the bush. I scramble for it, kind of wanting to rub my elbow but knowing I shouldn't. Not in front of them.

I drag the ball out of the bush, dribble it a little, and take a shot. It hits the rim at least. I make it in on the rebound and pass it off to Filipe. He gives me a weird look when he catches the ball. What's up with him today?

"Nice wheels," Theo says to me.

Nice wheels?

"The bike. Across the street. That thing your dad's?"

I catch Filipe's eye. Wait a sec to see if he's going to say something. Does Theo really not know? But then I remember that he only moved here two years ago, after it happened.

"A friend of my mom's," I say, wishing I could believe that's all Phil is.

"Too bad. That ride is sick. Someday I'm going to own a Harley."

Filipe goes back for a three-pointer. *Swoosh.* "Oh yeah," he says. "The Flip is back."

The Flip?

He's still barely said a word to me since I came over here. Almost like he's embarrassed of me, or something. Even though I made my shot for once.

Filipe tosses the basketball to Theo, who dribbles it through his legs and then goes up to dunk it. Such a show-off. Sure, he's tall. He's also a whole year older than us. Filipe and I are still waiting for our growth spurts.

"Hey, Filipe," I say.

He doesn't respond.

"Flip?" I try again.

He jogs toward me, but he doesn't look happy about it. "Theo invited himself over for . . ." He stops for a second, panting. "For one-on-one."

One-on-one.

He glances back at Theo, who's shooting a basket. The ball clangs off the rim, echoing loudly in my head.

"Oh," I say. "I get it." I turn for my own yard, swallowing down the things I can't say back. All the times we let Filipe join in on our plans. Tagging along with Mom and Xan and me when we went to the beach. Or coming over to my house on family movie night, insisting we rewatch all the Star Wars movies. We didn't do invites. We never needed to. *One-on-one?* Since when?

I stand at the edge of the driveway, waiting to cross the street.

"Hey, Theo," Filipe shouts, and I turn my head to watch. "Bet I can make this shot from all the way back here." The distance is way, way longer than a three. There's no way he'll make that shot. The odds are beyond against him.

Theo bounce-passes the ball. Filipe bends his

knees. He's like a spring, all that energy about to shoot out from his fingertips.

Still, there's no way he's making that shot.

My eyes follow the ball. Filipe's do too.

Swish.

"Wooo-hoo! Nothin' but net, baby." He jogs over to high-five Theo.

All I can do is stare at the ball, bouncing on the pavement. The ball that swished through that hoop seconds ago, like it was effortless. My best friend who told me to scram. Like it was effortless.

What am I doing still standing here, anyway? Looking on while Theo passes his Gatorade off to Filipe. From here, I can't tell if it's an optical illusion, or if Filipe actually grew a few inches in the night. Sorry—*the Flip.*

I cross the street. In my front yard, my brother is helping Phil shine his motorcycle.

One-on-one.

Sometimes Dad would take Xan or me out to do something special separately. Father-son one-on-one time, he called it. Sounds cheesy, I know, but I liked it. He let me choose where to go, too. Mini-golfing or a Paw Sox game or out to the movies. Mini-golf was my favorite. The place we went had a pirate theme and Dad would try to talk like a pirate the entire time, even when he paid the attendant at the beginning.

It would take us forever to finish because Dad would always say something ridiculously pirate-y just as I was about to swing and then I'd miss the ball entirely. One time, he made me laugh so hard I accidentally dropped my club into the water. We had to pay extra afterward for someone to fish it out, but Dad never told Mom when she asked if anything exciting happened. He just winked at me when she wasn't looking.

Xander peers up at Phil with this look on his face that I haven't seen in forever. Is that how I used to look up to Dad?

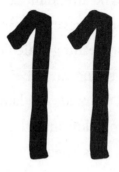

AFTER DINNER, MOM INVITES PHIL

to come to the park with us. We go a lot in the summer after supper, when it's finally cooling down. There's this loop Mom likes to walk—to help herself unwind, she says—but most of the time Xan and I do our own thing. There's a playground with a swing set, a koi pond, and a bandstand for when they have concerts in the summer.

A lot of the time, Filipe comes with us and we'll bring a Frisbee or a baseball to toss around, but after what happened a couple hours ago, I don't even bother to invite him. Don't want to get in the way of his one-on-one time with Theo.

It's not that I need to have Filipe all to myself or anything. He can be friends with whoever he wants. I just don't get what the big deal was today—why it *needed* to be one-on-one. And anyway, if somehow it did, why couldn't he find some way to say it, instead of being a jerk while waiting for me to figure it out?

Filipe and I used to be able to just tell each other stuff. But now it feels like there's stuff he's not saying—that he's purposely leaving out. And at the same time, he's mad at me for not being able to read his mind.

When we get out of the car at the park, Xan's about to run off to the playground like usual when Mom says, "Hey, hey, not so fast." Xan stops in his tracks. "I thought we could walk the loop together. The four of us, I mean."

The four of us? I don't exactly want Mom to walk the loop alone with Phil. But the alternative might be worse.

"Can I look for sticks?" Xan perks up. "And rocks?"

"Absolutely," Mom says. "But you can only bring one of each back. Got it?"

I have a feeling Xan will push back on this later, but for now he says, "Got it."

All I want to do is lag behind them, be Xan's two extra arms for holding sticks and rocks, but Phil isn't making that easy.

"Heard you were the hero at the library today, Drew."

"What? No I wasn't," I say, shoving my hands in my pockets as Phil slows down so that he's next to me while Mom helps Xander with a stick that's too big.

"So modest," he says. "Just like—" He clears his throat. *Just like who?* I wonder, but he doesn't leave me room to ask. "Anyway, so your mom says you're a big reader, too. Makes sense, I guess. All that time around books. What's your favorite? Or favorites? I know it's not easy to choose just one."

"I don't know," I say, even though of course I do. Right now it's a tie between *Holes* and *The Hobbit*. I've reread both so many times my copies are falling apart.

"Well, what've you read recently that you liked?"

How come he needs to know so badly? In a day or two he's going to leave town and I'll never have to see him again. Right? That's how Mom explained this whole deal to me, but suddenly I don't feel so sure about any of it. If he's got a thing for Mom, what if he—what if he stays?

"I said I don't know, all right?"

A snap as Xander's branch breaks. Mom turns back. "Drew," she says sharply.

"Sorry," I mumble.

"It's okay," Phil says.

I wish he would speed up or fall back behind, but it's like the dude can't take a hint. Maybe I need to ask him the right prying question. Something to get him off my back.

"Do you have kids?" I ask. "Or a wife? Or a husband?" I add quickly, covering all the bases. You never know.

"Drew, that's enough." Mom's holding a big stick, and while she's only holding it because of Xan, I decide to knock it off for now. We've still got a ways to go till we finish the loop.

"No, no, that's okay. It's all right to be curious," Phil says. "I'm not married, but I'd like to have a family someday. Be a father." He glances ahead at Mom for a second, but she's not looking back at him. She's making sure Xan doesn't run too fast with two sticks in his hands.

For a bit there, Phil goes quiet until Xan makes him carry a few sticks because he's trying to decide which is his favorite. I try to pull out my cell phone and play a game, but Mom notices and makes me put it away.

The funny thing is, for the whole loop, even though it's the four of us, it feels like Phil keeps trying to talk to me more than anyone else. Maybe he thinks it's a challenge. I'm the one person who doesn't want to be his pal, so he's going to keep at it, relentlessly, until I change my mind.

Unless it's something else.

After spending the night tossing and turning, I lie awake as the sun comes up. Between the curry Phil made for dinner and all that weirdness with Filipe, it was impossible to sleep.

Sure, he and Theo are on the soccer team together and the whole team went to camp last week for some kind of team-building thing. But Theo is older. He doesn't even go to the same school as us. And I heard a rumor that he goes to parties with high schoolers. So why does he suddenly want to hang out with Filipe?

Since when did Filipe become cool enough to hang out with Theo?

It doesn't make sense. None of it does. Not one part of this summer.

At least I don't have to worry about Audrey anymore.

I'm lying facedown on my pillow when I hear that sound again. Not the birds chirping. And not the sound of a motorcycle either. That unmistakable squeak of the sliding glass door opening. And then the clapping. The feet clomping on the ground.

I pull the pillow around my ears to block out the sound—the reminder of Phil's existence in our house—except it doesn't work. There's a part of me—my inner brain or whatever—that won't shut up. That needs to know *why* he's doing it.

My alarm clock reads 5:35. Mom is still asleep in her bedroom—will be for at least another hour. I tiptoe by Xan's room, where the door is ajar. His arms are hanging off the side of the bed, his face planted into a pillow. Typical Xan.

Downstairs, I pull open the sliding glass door that leads out to the back patio.

There he is, except he isn't doing jumping jacks

anymore. I don't know what to call what he's doing except being a weirdo. His feet turn in and out as he jumps side to side. His arms are up in the air, flailing. If it weren't for the fact that he's like, six-two and in pretty good shape, I'd say he could be mistaken for someone in a senior-citizen aerobics class at the Y.

I step off the patio and onto the dewy grass and clear my throat.

He keeps doing it.

I clear my throat again, this time louder. "Eh. Hem."

Nothing! He's either in the zone or doing his very best job of ignoring me.

"*What* are you doing?"

This time he stops. Feet flat on the ground. He tamped down that whole area of grass with his jumping.

He wears a big stupid grin on his face. "Hey, Drew."

"What are you doing?" I ask again, scratching a bug bite on my elbow.

"Do you want to give it a try?"

I shake my head. "Not really. Can you just . . . I mean, what are you even doing? And why do you have to do it? Every. Single. Morning?" Okay, two mornings in a row. But still. Clearly there's a pattern here.

"Whew! One question at a time, buddy. And while

you're at it, can you let a man catch his breath?" He smiles again.

I do not smile back.

"I'm trying to think of the best way to explain it, but I think that's just it. You can't completely explain it. You need to try it to see."

"No thanks."

Phil stares at me, still catching his breath.

"You know, you look like a weirdo when you do it." I imagine Filipe—or worse, Theo—catching me out here, jumping around in my pajamas with Phil, and what they'd say.

Phil laughs. "I'll bet. You know what—that's why I do it now, in the wee hours of the morning before anyone's awake. No one can see me. Well, except . . ." He gestures to me.

Does he know I watched yesterday?

"I'll close my eyes. Heck, I'll turn around. No one's watching you," he says. "Promise."

There's something about the way he looks at me, almost like how the kids stare up at me right before I begin a puppet show. And for some reason, this time I can't say no.

"Fine," I say. "But you have to turn around."

He does. "You gotta get warmed up first. Try hopping a little bit. Keep your feet just an inch or so off the ground. I'll do it too."

I do what he says. I hop. Once and then again, my feet barely clearing the grass. I feel stupid, and I swear someone is watching us, but I peek for a second, and the backyard is as empty as it was when I came out. Next thing I know, we're going higher, higher and higher until we're no longer hopping but full-on jumping. Our arms, waving in the air. Our ankles, turning in and out, in and out.

My feet hop left and right, left and right. My heart thumps loudly in my chest as the ground seems to shake beneath my feet. And soon that's all I can hear. The thumping on the ground, the pounding of my heart. My breath.

"Feels good, huh?" Phil asks.

I'm totally panting now. Maybe? All I know for sure is I definitely don't feel as much like an idiot as I thought I would at the start. "I guess?"

"Okay, we'll keep going for another couple minutes."

It's like I can actually feel the blood pumping through my body. Out from my heart and into my lungs, my arms and legs, my head, my feet, my stomach.

"Aaaand stop."

My heels hit the ground.

"Turn your palms out."

The slightest breeze tickles my upturned palms.

"And breathe."

My whole body feels tingly now that I've stopped moving. I don't even mean to, but I smile.

"Pretty amazing, huh?"

I'm not ready to give Phil the satisfaction he's looking for. "It feels all right."

Finally I turn and face Phil.

"So," Phil says, "you asked me why I do it."

"And?"

"I do it every morning because . . . well, because as you can probably see, it makes me feel alive. For a few moments, I like feeling my whole glorious body working for me. It's an amazing thing, life, and I don't want to ever forget."

The smile on my face is gone. I chew on the inside of my cheek. What's he trying to say? That *I* don't think life is amazing? That if I don't jump outside in my pajamas every morning like a weirdo, someday I'm going to do what Dad did?

He has no right—none at all—to come into our house and act like he knows everything. What does he think he's doing, anyway, coming all the way out here from Colorado? Does he think he's got some magical solution to fix my family? Fix me? That he's got it all figured out? Because he doesn't.

My ears get hot, and before I can manage to say any of that to him, I'm darting across the patio and slamming the sliding glass door behind me. The glass rattles so hard I think for a second it might fall out of the door and shatter into a million pieces. It doesn't, but it should.

Maybe it'd wake Mom up, wake her up from all this. Phil in our house, taking Dad's place for a couple days? It doesn't change what happened. Nothing ever will.

But there's something else rattling too.

My heart, which was beating so hard for the past ten minutes, is now constricting. Banging around in there. The empty cage of my ribs.

NONE OF IT WAKES UP MOM, THOUGH.

Instead I lie in my bed, my heart pounding for a few minutes, before I somehow fall asleep.

The next thing I know, Mom is rubbing my shoulder. "Drew?"

I pry my mouth off the pillow and wipe at some drool crusted around the corners of my mouth. Man, I must've really been out.

"I let you sleep in, but we need to get out the door soon."

I glance at the clock. How is it already eight fifteen?

I scramble out of bed, fumbling through my drawers for clean clothes.

In her dress shoes, Mom tip-taps out of my room and down the hallway.

Clean boxers, shirt, shorts, socks. I wet down the sticking-up parts of my hair in the bathroom and brush my teeth fast. And then I linger at the top of the stairs, the smells from the kitchen wafting up. Sausage and eggs. Hash browns?

Did Phil tell Mom what happened earlier this morning? He must have. That's the only explanation. The only reason she'd let me sleep in.

I start down the stairs.

Waiting for me at the edge of the kitchen counter is a brown paper bag. It doesn't have my name on it, but I know it's mine all the same. Phil is already putting the breakfast dishes into the dishwasher.

"There's a plate for you at the table." Phil turns as he hears me enter the room. "Xan tipped me off about sausage and eggs being your favorite."

Mom looks at me. What am I supposed to do? Just gobble up this food because he made it for me?

"I already brushed my teeth," I say.

Mom's face falls.

"And we need to go. Don't you have a meeting this morning?"

Mom claps her hand to her mouth. "Oh my gosh, you're right, Drew. I completely forgot. Can you track down your brother and make sure he's brushed his teeth before we head out the door? Don't want him breathing sausage breath all over the Y staff."

As I try to convince Xan to turn off the TV and brush his teeth, I can hear Mom and Phil in the kitchen.

"Who's the parent, huh?" Mom laughs. "Sheesh. Almost late to the meeting *I'm* in charge of. Good grief."

"You've got a lot on your plate, Kay."

"A lot *distracting* me." More laughter.

I can't get my brother up the stairs fast enough.

As I make my way down the back staircase to the children's room, I'm still holding the brown paper lunch bag in my hand. I haven't opened it to see what's inside. Not that it matters. Whatever's in there, it's not headed for my stomach. I'd rather go hungry.

The children's room is empty. Mrs. Eisenberg is in the meeting upstairs with all the other librarians. I crunch the brown paper bag in my hand, squishing the sandwich and whatever else is inside, and chuck it into the metal garbage can in the corner of the room. *Clang.*

A gasp.

"Audrey?" I say.

She stands up from a beanbag chair over by the fiction section and pulls out her earbuds.

"I didn't realize anyone else was down here." I chew on my lip.

"What was that noise?"

I glance at the trash can. "Just throwing something away."

"Was it *alive?*"

"Huh?"

Audrey huffs as she walks toward me, her earbuds swinging from her hand. "All I'm saying is, that's an awful lot of noise to make just throwing something in the garbage."

I shrug.

"Are you okay?" Audrey waits for an answer.

In the back of the room, that stupid light above the aquarium is buzzing again. You'd think I would like the quiet. The space from Phil. But it's like no matter where I go, he comes with me anyway.

"I'm fine!" I say, grabbing the cutting project from yesterday and slamming it down on the table.

Audrey tucks some hair behind her ears. I guess maybe I could've said it a little more like a person who was *actually* fine.

She sits down in the chair across from me. I can already tell she's one of those people who sits on only part of the chair, like she's waiting for a friend to fill up the other half, which is funny, because I wouldn't have guessed someone like Audrey really has that many friends.

"There's this guy," I say. "He's staying with us for a little while."

"A guy? Like a teenager?"

I shake my head. "Way older. Like forty."

Audrey tilts her head. "What about your dad?"

I want to slam my head on the table. My dad. What I'd told Audrey two days ago. "He doesn't live with us anymore."

Audrey considers this for a second. It's not a lie, exactly. "So, this guy. What is it about him that makes you want to toss garbage into the trash can with a murderous rage?"

"It wasn't—"

"Drew, people *upstairs* could hear that noise."

"Oh."

"Do you think this guy is having an affair with your mom?"

"What? No." Don't those only happen on TV shows? When Filipe's vovó used to babysit him, she was always watching soap operas where everyone was having affairs. My mom can't have an affair, though. Not that I can explain that to Audrey. For her to have an affair, Dad would have to be alive.

"It's not that crazy of a question," she says. "It happens all the time. At least, it does at universities. I overheard my mom and dad talking about one of their friends who was having one and—"

"Audrey."

"What?"

"I thought you wanted to help."

"Oh."

Why I ever thought that in the first place, I don't know. I mean, this is Audrey. For all I know, her friends before me were cats. It wouldn't be the most surprising thing.

Wait, did I just call Audrey a *friend*?

"So, the official reason he's here is that he's on

this motorcycle trip across the country, right? But I've never even heard of him before. My mom said he's her 'old friend,' but he's definitely acting like he likes her. Helping around the house and stuff. Being all nice to Xan. Trying to be all nice to me, not that it's working. It just seems fishy. Like, why? Why now? What's he expecting to happen, you know?"

"Okay, okay. So . . . what do you want? I mean, what would help with this guy—wait, what's his name?"

"Oh, get ready for it."

"One sec." Audrey pulls a ChapStick out of her pocket and slathers it on her lips. I'm not sure what about this moment requires ChapStick, but okay. "I'm ready," she says once she's finished.

"Phil . . . Pittman."

Audrey snorts.

"Audrey!"

"His name is *really* Phil Pittman?"

"Really."

Audrey glances over at the bank of computers. "Did you look him up yet?"

"What do you mean?"

"You know, google him. Figure out who you're dealing with."

I shake my head. Why hadn't I thought of googling him? That's the kind of thing Filipe and I would've done right away any other summer.

"What are we waiting for?"

I check the clock. We still have another ten minutes until Mrs. Eisenberg will be back from her meeting. And the room *is* empty. And, okay, even if Mrs. Eisenberg does come down and we're on the computer, it's not like we'll be in trouble. She's not exactly paying us.

Audrey jumps up and is on that thing before I've even answered. She sits on half of the chair like she's expecting me to sit on the other half. Nuh-uh. I roll over another chair.

She waves her fingers above the keyboard like a magician.

"Audrey . . ."

"Okay, Phil Pittman," she says. "Show us your true self."

She types his name into the search bar and clicks the blue button.

13

FOUR HUNDRED NINETY-NINE THOUSAND.

"Yikes," I say.

"That's a whole lot of Pittmans."

"How are we ever going to find mine?" *Mine.* I shudder. "I mean, the real one."

"Easy peasy," Audrey says. She sounds like my grandmother. Maybe her only real friends *are* grandmothers. "What else do you know about him?"

"Um."

"Oh, come on. Like, where's he from? Where'd he go to college? Has he ever been convicted of a felony?"

She switches over to image search, and suddenly dozens of Phil Pittmans fill the screen. One with a legit wizard beard. One with wire glasses sort of like Dad's. A mug shot. And another with scary face tattoos. Guess my mom could have invited a weirder Phil Pittman into our home.

"Are any of these guys him?"

"Nope."

"You really don't know anything about him? Come on, Drew. I mean, how'd he get to your house? Did you see his license plate?"

I did catch it the other day. Green with white mountains. Plus, he went to the same high school as Mom. "Colorado."

Audrey drops the mouse. "Wait—Colorado? What's he doing all the way on the East Coast? Hmmmmm. Long bike trip. Far from home. What if there's something he's running away from?" Audrey's eyebrows shoot up.

Whoa. She's onto something. I lean in. "This whole thing—it's weird, right?"

"Very." She goes back to the search bar and enters *Phil Pittman* and *Colorado*.

He isn't the only Phil Pittman in Colorado, it turns

out. But we're getting closer. I can feel it. And Audrey must be feeling something too, because as she scrolls down the page, I can hear her breathing through her nose. Short, fast breaths, like how Filipe's dog Tobey breathes when he's having a nightmare.

And then I see the headline: ONE MAN'S CROSS-COUNTRY MOTORCYCLE JOURNEY AND THE INSPIRATION BEHIND IT.

"That's him!"

"Which one?" The cursor shoots across the page.

"The motorcycle one, right there." I press my fingertip to the screen. When I pull away, it leaves a smudge on the glass.

Audrey clicks on the article. Now it's me doing the nightmare-dog-breath thing.

"'It's a warm spring day in rural Iowa when Phil Pittman pulls up on his Harley and—'"

"Audrey, stop! I can read, you know."

"Okay. Sheesh."

I tell her when to scroll down, and she does. I can hardly believe it. Some news reporter from Iowa interviewed Phil back in April about his motorcycle trip. He's spending the whole year riding his bike across the country—every state except Alaska and Hawaii.

So that's why Mom couldn't answer where he was living. For the whole year, his home is the open road. The bike ride is a fund-raiser on behalf of his brother, who—who died, named . . . Andrew.

When I get to that part, I stop reading. If it were my finger on the mouse, I'd have closed the whole website. The browser, too. And walked away. But it's Audrey's hand on the mouse, not mine.

All I hear in my head is Phil's voice. What he said early this morning. *It's an amazing thing, life.*

"Can I scroll down more?" she asks.

"Uh-huh."

I'm not supposed to have anything in common with Phil. But I do. He lost someone he loved too. *Andrew.*

Phil's brother's name is the same as mine. That's a little strange, right? I'm the only Andrew in my entire grade at school. I know my name's not that rare, but still.

Audrey's eyes are so glued to the screen she doesn't notice that I've stopped reading. That my gaze has shifted to the posters on the wall. That Darth Vader READ poster. Like *he* really sat around reading.

I lean my chair back from the computer just as the

elevator door opens. Mrs. Eisenberg pushes out a full cart of books. "Lot of returns in the late bin and our page is out sick," she says. "Audrey, you think you can give me a hand here?"

Audrey goes over to help.

"Actually, Drew, as I was heading out the door last night, I noticed someone did a real number on the easy readers. Could you tidy up that section before story hour? It'd be a huge help."

"Sure," I say, still thinking about that newspaper article and Phil's brother, Andrew.

When I round the corner toward the easy readers, I see that Mrs. Eisenberg isn't kidding. Did a kid pull these off the shelf or was it an EF-5 tornado? They aren't in any order at all, so I'll have to start from scratch.

I pull out a whole misfiled section and begin putting them in order by author.

Are You My Mother? by P. D. Eastman.

As I stare at the book in my hand, I feel suddenly kind of light-headed. Is it just me or did someone make the lights in here brighter? The buzzing, it sounds too loud.

Mom used to read this book to me all the time when I was little. That little baby bird, wandering around, asking everyone if they're its mom. A kitten, a cow—even an airplane. It used to make me laugh and laugh, because how could a bird be so stupid as to not know who its mother is? It's a bird, dummy.

But right now, the whole thing only makes me woozy.

In my head, all I see is that strange look Phil gave me when he first appeared at my house and I told him my name was Andrew. That sort of smile, almost like he had a secret.

What if he did have one?

Come to think of it, Mom had that smile too the night that Phil came. *Now's not the time to tell him.* She said that, on the stairs that night, to Phil. *He's not ready yet.*

The *he* . . . it's *me*. It is, isn't it?

When I asked Phil yesterday if he had any kids, he didn't answer the question. No, now that I'm really thinking about it, it's so clear. He dodged it. He said he wanted a family someday. Wanted to be a father.

Someday. Like now?

I knew it didn't make sense—him showing up all of a sudden. Mom never saying anything about his trip to us before. An *old friend* who's close enough to come and stay in our house, but that we've never heard of? It doesn't add up.

Except maybe it does.

If he's just some friend passing through town, how come he keeps trying to connect with *me*? Like this morning, when he was doing his crazy exercise routine. And on that walk last night. If he's here for Mom, why wouldn't he just talk to her and ignore me and Xan? And heck, if he's here because he wants to be part of *our* family *someday*, why all the focus on me? It's way easier to get close to Xan. My brother's the friendliest little kid on the planet. He's BFFs with half the staff at Panera.

No, he's not just here for Mom. That's obvious. But what if he's here for . . . for me?

Before Dad died, Mom used to joke that I was her mini-me while Xan was all Dad. Dad's stick-straight brown hair. Dad's restless sleeping. Dad's love of all things history. What did I get from Dad anyway? It's not like Dad could cook. He was basically useless in the kitchen. At Thanksgiving, Mom would put him in charge of mashed potatoes like it was a seriously big deal, and even then they always came out either lumpy or soupy.

But Phil cooks. Phil *loves* to cook.

Like me.

What if I'm not half-Dad at all? What if—

No.

No.

Is that why my name is Andrew? Did Mom name me in honor of Phil's dead brother because Phil's really my—

I press a hand to my forehead. It doesn't feel hot.

What if *I'm* the real reason Phil came here?

I want to pinch myself. This is not real life. No way.

But maybe?

Maybe.

That ball in my throat is back again.

What if Dad isn't actually my real dad?

My palms leave little sweat streaks on the front cover of *Are You My Mother?* I wipe the book on my pants, trying to dry them off.

What if my *real* dad is Phil?

NO. NO WAY. THAT'S . . . IT'S CRAZY.

But the thing is, maybe it's not. It would definitely explain why he's here. And why Mom was so weird about it. It's not exactly an easy thing to do—bring by the guy who's your son's real father.

Though why now? Why did it take him this long?

I sit down on the floor, giving my wobbly knees a break, and turn back to see what Audrey and Mrs. Eisenberg are up to. Audrey's tongue sneaks out of the corner of her mouth. She's deep in concentration as she puts the books in order by Dewey decimal number.

Mrs. Eisenberg is at her computer, flipping through a magazine.

I turn back to the mess in front of me and take a deep breath.

Phil can't *be my dad.* It's biologically impossible.

But what about what Audrey said just a few minutes ago? *Affairs happen all the time.* What if Dad never even knew? What if Xander's not really my brother? What if—

Okay, now my hand's trembling too. I grab onto the cool metal edge of the bookshelf and grip it hard. *Get it together, Drew.* Then I start laughing. A laugh I can't control. Xander and I have the same mom. He's still my brother, no matter what. *Sheesh, Drew. Come on!*

"What are you laughing about?" Audrey asks from across the room.

"Nothing." I pop my head up for a second. "Just a funny book."

Audrey huffs. "Are you done putting the easy readers in order yet? This cart is huge and we need to shelve it before the first story hour."

The easy readers still look like a tornado hit them. "Be there in a sec," I yell back, quickly grabbing the *A*s and *B*s and slapping them on the shelf.

The thing is, though, the more I think about Phil being my dad, the more it starts to almost make sense. There was so much that Dad wasn't truthful about. Maybe he always knew he wasn't my real dad, but he played along—pretended—that he was. Just another one of his lies.

The possible truths stretch out, bending and branching off like limbs on some gnarled, twisted old tree.

Still, there's this one thought about Phil being my real dad that I can't let go of. That simmers on the back burner of a very crowded stove in my mind. I don't even know what to do with it, but it's there all the same. If Phil were my real dad, that would mean my real dad didn't kill himself. That no part of someone who could do that to himself was in my DNA. I wouldn't have to worry about turning into him anymore.

That's the one thought that gives me relief.

For the rest of the day at the library, I keep these thoughts a secret. I mean, it's not like I can just say, *Hey, so Audrey, I think my birth dad might not actually be my real dad. And remember that guy we just Google-stalked this morning? I think it's him. Plus, I lied to you and my real dad is dead.*

Even Audrey would do that slow, slightly terrified backward walk in order to get away from me as quickly as possible before never talking to me ever again.

You can't say that kind of stuff to anyone. Period.

Instead I spend the rest of the morning and afternoon thinking about it. The kind of thinking that takes up nearly all of your brain power and makes you do stupid things, like walking into the women's restroom instead of the men's room and not knowing what's so weird until you're asking an old lady using the hand dryer about where the urinals went and she gives you a look like you've got two heads.

Yeah. It's been that kind of afternoon.

By the time I get in the car with Mom to head home for the day, I'm ready to collapse into my bed. I'm all thunk out.

I'm clicking my seat belt into the buckle when I notice Mom staring at me. "What?" I ask.

"You're looking at me funny," she says.

"No, I'm not. *You* were just looking at *me* funny."

"Only because . . ." Mom places her hands on the wheel and sighs. "Okay, fine. Maybe I was. But it's just—you're awfully quiet for the end of the day."

I shrug.

"It's fine, really. I don't need you to talk. Honestly, after a whole afternoon of listening to Loretta on the phone trying to find a new podiatrist, I can't say I mind the quiet." Mom shares an office with Loretta, and Loretta's always driving her crazy.

The quiet doesn't last long. A few minutes later, we pick Xander up from the Y and he's talking enough for the both of us. Telling us all about how Sammy Weathers puked right after afternoon snack and how the puke looked, in great detail.

"You know, I think we've had enough—" Mom tries to cut in.

"No, Mom, I haven't gotten to the best part yet."

The best part of a barf story? Okay, now I'm a little intrigued.

But just as we're pulling into our driveway, Xander cuts his tale short. "Wait! Where's Phil's motorcycle?"

Mom turns the car off, glancing at my brother in the rearview mirror. "I'm so sorry you didn't get to say goodbye to him, hon—"

"He's gone?" Xander's smile evaporates.

He's gone.

"He swung by the library around lunchtime to say goodbye. We're in such a nice stretch of weather, he decided to head up the coast for the next week—"

"No fair." Xander crosses his arms. "He said he was going to take me on his motorcycle."

"Well." Mom reaches for her purse in the back seat. "We never discussed that, actually. And anyway, he'd need to put on a car seat of some sort and you'd need a helmet and—"

He's gone. I stare out the window at the grass he was mowing just yesterday, the lines already fading. How can he be gone already when I still need to know who he really is to me? There's a pinch in my gut. *Maybe he wouldn't have left if you'd been nicer to him, Drew. Maybe he'd still be here, or at least have come downstairs to say goodbye.*

Xander's opening his car door and running across the yard.

"They form attachments so easily at that age." Mom undoes her own buckle, turning to me. "Not like you."

"What's that supposed to mean?" I step outside and stretch my arms above my head. Xander's still yammering on and on about how bummed he is to not ride the motorcycle.

Mom shuts her door. "Just that . . ."

"What?"

"Never mind," she says quietly as we head toward the garage. "In any case, *you* must be thrilled."

"Thrilled?"

"You didn't exactly hide your feelings about Phil."

"Yeah, well, maybe you should've asked me and Xander before turning our house into a hotel. It's not fair for Xan, you know? Having new people come and go like that. He's just a kid."

Mom fumbles with the key. "I'd hardly call it a hotel, Drew." She pushes the door open. "Hey, who's the parent here, anyway?" She says it with a smile, like it's the kind of question that isn't actually a question. What's that called again? Oh right. A rhetorical question.

But I have a different answer. "I don't know sometimes," I mumble.

Mom slams her keys down on the counter, startling me. "I've had about enough of that attitude. Now, I let some of your behavior slide because Phil was here, but that's not the case anymore. I'd hate to have to take your cell phone away."

"I'm sorry."

She slides off her dress shoes and slips into a pair of flip-flops, rubbing at her temples. "I've got a bit of a headache. Loretta, you know? I'm going to lie down before supper. You mind keeping an eye on your brother?"

"Fine," I say, knowing there's no other acceptable answer.

Mom heads up the stairs without another word. As I fill up a glass of water at the sink, I peer out the kitchen window into the backyard.

Xan bounces a tennis ball on the patio. *Bop, bop, bop.* With each bounce, a different question pops into my head. Was it me who scared off Phil? *Bop.* Why did he show up now? *Bop.* Will he come back? *Bop.* Can I have a second chance? *Bop.*

He counts as he keeps going, but then at seven he loses the ball and has to start the count all over again. He catches me in the window. "Drew, I did ten! In a row! Do you think I can do twenty?"

"Let's see," I tell him through the screen.

As I'm watching, I think I hear something. Is Mom on the phone upstairs? I pretend I'm watching Xan when really I'm straining to hear what she's saying.

He fumbles the ball right after sixteen in a row.

"Hey, Xan?"

"Yeah?"

"I have to pee. I'll be right back."

"After, can you come outside? I'm bored."

"Sure."

I don't go to the bathroom like I said I would. Instead I creep up the stairs, slowly, so they don't creak. Halfway up I stop and sit.

"It just felt so right, Jules. It's hard to explain."

Mom's voice goes quiet.

"But then he left. And all rushed like that? What does that mean? I'm too old. I'm not good at this. I don't remember how to play these games."

Games?

"I know, I know. It's just . . . he was so good with Xan. But you should've seen him with Drew, Jules. They're so alike it kills me."

My stomach drops. Falls into the deepest pit inside me.

"I know. I need to tell him. I've been waiting for the right moment, but it's hard."

Is she saying what I think she's saying?

It's impossible to stay still on the stairs when I feel like I'm jumping out of my own skin. *So alike it kills me.* Me and Phil?

"No, you're right. He asked if he could stop by

again when he's finished his New England loop."

So he is coming back. Here. My heart slows back to normal. I still have a chance with him.

"Oh? Go, go, I don't want to get in the way of your dinner. We can catch up later. I'm—I'm fine. Really. Okay. Okay. Bye, Jules."

And then it goes quiet again, the only sound the faint *bop-bop* of the tennis ball on the patio. Xan's probably wondering where I went, but I can't budge. I'm stuck in place, trying to imagine how it'll be when he comes back. I can't ask him point-blank. If he's not my dad, he'll think I'm delusional for ever thinking he could be. Mom too. I need to find some way that's natural.

The wooden floorboards creak under Mom's steps. And then I hear her body hit the bed.

It's the next sound that I don't expect. I heard it so many times in that first year that I'll never, ever forget it.

A muffled sob.

Back then I would stroke her hair, rub her shoulder. The same things her friends did when she got like that. I didn't know it was weird. It was what she needed, but now, looking back on it, it's a little weird.

A kid comforting his own mom? It's supposed to be the other way around.

Did she lie too?

All those years, could she have tricked me? She would have known too, right, if Phil were my dad?

I don't know what to believe anymore. Has my whole life been a lie?

The kitchen door opens, slamming against the wall. "Drew?"

I'm down the stairs so fast, a finger to my lip. "Mom's got a headache."

"Oh." Xan lowers his voice. "Sorry. But you were taking forever and you only said a pee. Did you do number two? You did, didn't you? You never, ever, ever say you do, but you do, otherwise you'd explode."

"You got me. I'm the biggest liar ever." I hold my hands up. Guilty as charged.

Except my lie wasn't big at all.

Not nearly as big as Dad's lies. And maybe Mom's, too.

YOU KNOW HOW WHEN YOU WAKE

up in the morning, there's a second—okay, maybe it's longer than that, but it's not as long as a minute—so there's some time where you're just lying in bed and you're not really awake and it's almost like the world isn't real. You don't know who you are or what's going on. You're barely existing. Caught in the space between the dream world and the real world, even if it only lasts twenty seconds.

And then something real hits you. Maybe it's *Oh my gosh, I have a test today*, and your heartbeat picks up. Or maybe it's *Yessssss, it's Saturday, no school!*

And maybe sometime, if you're really unlucky, it's that your dad is gone. He's gone and he's never coming back. And even worse than that: he left you. And it takes your breath away. You don't really ever want to get out of bed, but you know you have to because your mom needs you. And your brother needs you. Your dad's gone, but the earth keeps rotating on its axis.

I wake up before my alarm the next day, and as I come out of that foggy haze, two things hit me.

One: maybe my dad isn't who I thought he was.

And two: Phil's gone. I scared him off.

Sunlight slants through the edges of my shade, hitting the *Star Wars: The Force Awakens* poster over my bureau. It's still quiet in the house. I flip over to check my alarm clock. Five thirty. Hours till I have to get up to go to the library. I slip out of bed, tiptoe over to my window, and lift up the shade.

The grass that Phil and I tamped down yesterday morning is wet with dew, sparkling in the morning sunlight. But the backyard looks empty now, which is weird because, really, it looks the same as it did three mornings ago, never mind all the mornings before. It's not like it *always* had a weirdo doing jumping jacks in it at the crack of dawn. I shake my head. Was one of those weirdos yesterday really me? Could that other weirdo have been my dad?

I climb back into bed and shut my eyes. Flip onto my stomach. Turn the pillow onto the cool side. But none of it helps me get back to sleep.

There's this weird tingly feeling in my legs. And, okay, maybe my arms, too. Almost like I want to be outside, shaking it all out.

But I don't want to do that.

That would be crazy.

Right?

Thing is, though, it's actually one of the less crazy thoughts running through my brain the past twenty-four hours.

Phil leaving was supposed to make everything go back to normal. But it doesn't. And not just because I miss him. He was only here for a few days—but I do. The house feels quieter now that he's left.

I can't let go of what I learned yesterday, about his brother being named Andrew too. Or what I over-heard Mom say on the phone.

It's not proof, of course. I didn't hear Mom's whole conversation with Julia or what Julia said to Mom.

That's what I need, though. *Proof.* Something concrete that shows he's my dad. Or that it's at least not completely crazy to think he might be. I can't go to Mom with less than that, or I'll look . . .

Fragile. Like how Dad supposedly was. Is that how people see me? Like if they say or do the wrong thing, I'll break?

Does Filipe ever think of me like that? Do other kids at school?

I always thought they just felt bad for me. Bad in that way you can't express with words. But maybe that's not exactly it.

Maybe the proof can come in the other direction too. Something irrefutable—I think that's the word, at least—that proves I'm Dad's son. That means my whole life hasn't been a lie. And then everything can truly go back to normal. At least the normal that's been my life for the past three years.

And then Phil can go back to being a kind of strange guy with an even stranger favorite way to exercise who stayed at our house for a few days and then went on his way. Nothing more than that.

I don't know which one's better. When Dad died, it rearranged my life completely. The past three years would've looked so different if he'd been around for them.

In those days after Dad died, all I wanted was some way to hit undo. Exit without saving progress. If Phil is my real dad, maybe I can undo. The hugest kind of undo. Erase all progress. Reboot and start over.

The morning at the library rushes by in a blur of story hour, giggly five-year-olds, smelly diapers, puppets, name tags, juice spills, and a table that's crusted over with glue no matter how many times Audrey and I wipe it down with a sponge. A happy distraction from thinking about Dad and Phil.

"You know what," Mrs. Eisenberg says, finally settling down into her chair at eleven forty-five a.m. as the last story-hour family gets on the elevator. "I think you two deserve a Del's."

Just hearing that word makes my mouth water.

"A Del's?" Audrey asks.

I almost fall out of my chair. "You've been in Rhode Island for how many weeks and you haven't had a Del's yet?"

"I don't know what it is," she says. "Hence my question."

Hence? Okay, Audrey.

"Well, then." Mrs. Eisenberg chuckles. "Better show her, Drew. Can't spend a summer in Rhode Island without having a Del's or two . . . or three dozen."

"Okay, can someone just tell me what it is?"

I catch Mrs. Eisenberg's eye. Nah. It's way too fun to give in now.

"Nope," she says, crossing her arms.

Audrey scrunches her face, fully aware I'm not going to give in.

"Come on!" I catch myself before grabbing her hand to help her out of her chair. That was close. Mrs. Eisenberg gives me a ten-dollar bill, and then I'm running for the door to the stairs. "You're going to love it."

"Debatable," Audrey says. Though she is following me, so that counts for something.

We make our way up the stairs and through the main room of the library. Mom's at the reference desk, but not with a patron right now. "Audrey and I are getting Del's. Do you want one?"

Mom's thinking about it. "Um, maybe later, bud. Thanks for asking."

I try to see if there's any hint of her crying last night, but she looks okay today. Normal.

"You're ridiculous, you know?" Audrey says as we step out into the sun. It's got to be at least ninety degrees outside. You're practically required to get a Del's when it's this hot. "I sure hope it's not something gross, like . . . chocolate-covered opossum on a stick."

The Del's truck is parked down the street a block. I lead us that way. "Wait a minute. *I'm* the ridiculous one? You just suggested a popular summertime treat in Rhode Island is chocolate-covered opossum."

"On a stick." I think I catch her almost giggle.

Turns out I'm not the only one thirsting after a Del's, so Audrey and I get into the line. "Lots of people excited about chocolate-covered opossum today," I say loud enough for the man in the black suit in front of us to raise an eyebrow.

Finally it's our turn. I step up to the truck. "Two mediums, please."

The man working the truck has a pretty sweet Mohawk. How long did it take him to get his hair that long? "Flavor?" he asks.

"Oh, lemon," I say. "Lemon for both."

"Hey, what if I don't want a lemon one?" Audrey peeks inside the truck.

"Trust me, you do. You can try the other flavors later, but cross my heart, you will go back to the lemon."

"Fiiiiine."

Mr. Mohawk trades us the two medium paper cups of freshly squeezed lemon-ice slushies for my ten dollars. I slip the change in my pocket, and Audrey and I walk over to some nearby benches in the shade.

"So, what do you think?" I ask as she's about to take her first slurp.

"I wish you'd let me get a straw so I could eat this like a normal person." She's tipping her cup at a scary angle and I picture the whole thing sloshing down onto her face.

"No!"

Audrey startles.

"Like this," I explain, squishing my cup to create a little spout for sipping.

"Oh," she says, copying me. "Oh! This is good!"

"Told you. See, not everything about Rhode Island is so bad."

"I never said that." She stops for a sec and holds her cup. I wonder if the brain freeze is setting in.

"Actually, you kind of did. That first day at the library."

"Yeah, well . . . I guess . . ." She takes another slurp. "Sometimes—very rarely—I am wrong about things. First impressions, you know?"

I know a thing about first impressions, I think, imagining Phil when I first met him, motorcycle helmet in hand. "Yeah," I say.

A chunk of the slushie falls onto my wrist. As I go to lick it off, I remember how little Devin Ferrera's hands were covered in glue earlier today and how Audrey super cautiously handed him a paper towel and wished him "Good luck with that mess" before running away from him.

"Hey, Audrey?"

"Yeah."

"How come you're so nervous when it comes to the kids? Like, did something happen once that made you scared, or . . ."

Audrey chews on the top of her cup for a second. "Maybe I wouldn't be this way if I had a little brother or a sister, but I don't. I guess I never figured out how to act around them. Plus, they're basically tiny germ factories with their boogery noses, plus poop and pee and barf coming out all the time."

"All the time?" I can't help it. I laugh. "There's a

big difference between a five-year-old and a newborn, Audrey."

She takes a sip of Del's. "Plus . . . I don't know. It's not so easy getting them to like you. Sure, you're a natural, but I swear, I tried to talk to a couple kids the other day after story hour and they stared back at me like I had an arm coming out of my head."

"Actually, if you did have an arm coming out of your head, I bet you'd be pretty popular with the kids from story hour. They love weird stuff like that."

"I guess I *could* try harder. . . . I mean, we've still got a few more weeks of July, plus all of August."

"How about this? If I see you doing a good job with the kids, I'll flash you a thumbs-up. And if it's not going too hot, I'll . . . um . . . I'll have a coughing fit!"

Audrey looks a little skeptical of my plan. "I guess it can't hurt," she says. "Sure."

We just sit there, letting the lemony goodness of Del's soak in and cool us off. Something changed between me and Audrey the other day when we looked up the stuff about Phil. She didn't hassle me about it the way Filipe would have. Maybe it's because she doesn't know everything about me the way he does.

We don't have so many years of shared history. I feel like I can trust her.

"Hey, Audrey?"

"Yeah."

I can't believe I'm about to say this. I can't. No. I shouldn't. Agghhh.

"You know how yesterday you said that thing about affairs?"

"Yeah?"

"I think . . ." I have to take another big slurp before I can say it out loud. "Maybe . . ."

"I can't understand you. Maybe you should swallow first before talking?"

I swallow. "Sorry. Sometimes I do this thing where"—I slosh a bunch more Del's into my mouth—"I need to eat to calm down." I swallow again. "Oooh. Too much Del's. Brain freeze."

"Okay, so all of what you just said? I understood about twenty percent of it."

"Right." I glance around in case somehow Mom or one of her library friends is nearby. The coast is clear. I have no other excuse now. This is my chance to say it. "I think there's a chance that Phil might be . . . my real dad."

I take another gulp of Del's right after I say it. The chill from the Del's has nothing on the relief that comes after saying the words out loud, finally, to someone. *Phil is my real dad.* The words ring in my ear. They don't sound half as bad as I thought they would. *Phil is my dad. My dad. Phil.*

Audrey's face goes all serious, and then I get it. If Phil somehow really is my dad, it is serious. Big-time serious. Maybe I didn't one hundred percent get that before, but I do now.

She takes another sip, crunching the ice with her teeth. My dad hated when I crunched on ice. Said it was super bad for my teeth. *My dad.* "Wait, though," Audrey says. "But why, why do you think *he* is? Phil, I mean."

"Remember that article you found yesterday, how it mentioned his dead brother, Andrew? *I'm* Andrew. I mean, Drew is short for Andrew. And he knew my mom, knew her before my dad. At first I thought it was just a crush, but maybe that isn't it. Maybe they dated in high school and never told my dad. Plus, he acted all weird the first time I met him. Ever since he came around, it seemed like he was trying to get to know me. Bond with me, you know? And earlier I heard him and my mom talking about how they had to tell me something, they just needed the right time. I didn't put it all together until yesterday, but—there's something going on here, Audrey. I know it. Some other reason he's here—it's not just what they said. I think it's me."

Audrey chews on that for a minute before taking another slurp of her Del's. "Okay, so . . . how would you prove it?"

"That's the thing. I don't even know where to start."

"Well, you know there's kits you can buy online, right? All you need is something with his DNA on it. A hair, or some spit."

"I don't have the dude's spit! And anyway, how much are those kits?"

Audrey shakes her cup. "A couple hundred dollars? A thousand?"

"I don't have that kind of money. Plus, I don't have his DNA. Not now, but . . ."

"What?"

"He left yesterday, but he's coming back after he rides up through Massachusetts, New Hampshire, Vermont, and Maine."

"How long will that take?"

I shrug.

They're so alike, it kills me. Did Mom mean we look alike, me and Phil? I can't imagine it. Phil is so hairy. And so . . . grown-up-looking. But when he was younger, maybe? Did he . . . did he look like me then? Do I look like a younger Phil?

Last year Filipe got this app for his phone that lets you do a face morph. You take a picture of yourself and morph it back into you as a baby, or morph it forward to you as an adult, or as an old person. Or as a girl if you're a boy. The results were hilarious. Filipe made a hideous girl. It's not an exact science, I guess. And of course Filipe kept having it morph his face with Tobey's.

If you morph me forward, would I look like Phil? If Phil got morphed backward, did you get me? Or something close?

If I could just find a picture of Phil from when he was younger, I'd know. I'd know if it was possible, at least. If our faces were on some continuum of Phil-ness or Drew-ness. I've seen pictures of my dad from when he was little. He looked just like Xan, nothing like me.

But where could I find a picture of Phil?

Audrey slurps out the last bit of her Del's. "Drew? What are you thinking?"

"Hold on." I start tearing at the soft, wet rim of my empty Del's cup. "If I could see pictures of Phil when he was younger, I'd be able to tell. He'd look like me. I'd look like him. Right?"

Audrey perks up. "Facebook?"

I shake my head. "He's too old. The pictures won't go back that far."

Audrey stares off into the distance, her brain in hyper speed. She almost jumps off the bench. "I know! His yearbook."

His yearbook. She's right. It's perfect—well, as perfect as I'm going to get without his DNA. "But how am I going to get his yearbook? His school was in Colorado."

"You said he went to school with your mom, right? So wouldn't he be in her yearbook? Have you looked at it before?"

I shake my head no. But that doesn't mean she doesn't have one. I've never looked. Never really had a need until now. Being a librarian, Mom's always been kind of a book hoarder. There's that big wall of shelves in our living room, plus the bookcases in her bedroom. And Xan and I have our own in our bedrooms. I swear, if there were more room, she'd have crammed some bookshelves into the bathroom. It's got to be on one of those shelves.

"I'll look for it when I get home." I crumple what's left of my Del's cup into a little ball and aim it for the trash can across the way. I make it in, easily. A three-point shot.

"You'll let me know what you find tomorrow, right?"

"Sure."

When Audrey smiles, I catch the tiniest piece of lemon rind stuck on her lip. "You have a little . . ." I point to my own lip.

Audrey swipes her hand across her mouth. "Gone?"

"Gone."

For a moment we're both quiet. A tiny thought flits through my brain: Audrey has no idea the real reason I want Phil to be my dad. How it wouldn't just change my past, but my future.

Back in fifth grade, we had this hero project. You had to write an essay about your personal hero, and then afterward there was this day where everyone in the whole grade dressed up like their hero, and pretended to be them for a whole day. You know how many kids chose their dads?

A lot.

It's not like Phil's the coolest guy on the planet or anything. I mean, the guy does do jumping jacks in his pajamas outside at the crack of dawn. But I bet if I got to know him, I'd find out more things that make him cool. Admirable, even. I mean, to start, he does have a motorcycle. And it's pretty brave to travel across the whole country by yourself.

It wouldn't be the worst thing in the world to end up like Phil when I'm older. For one, it would mean I'd still be alive.

I WATCH THROUGH MY BEDROOM

window as Mom's car backs out of the driveway. She's taking Xan to tae kwon do and running errands in between, which gives me about an hour to look for the yearbook. It's not a lot of time, but it should be enough.

I start in Mom's bedroom, since that'll be the hardest place to check later. It's tidy in here—a lot tidier than my room, anyway—except for when it comes to books. First, there's the pile on her bedside table, then the stack next to it that's got to be modeled on the

Leaning Tower of Pisa, and then there are the book-shelves.

For someone who works around books all day, you'd think she might want a break when she gets home. But I guess I can't exactly talk.

I start with the ones by her bedside table, since there are fewer of them. Plus, maybe she dug the year-book out knowing Phil was coming into town.

A novel by Curtis Sittenfeld, two cookbooks about tomatoes, a bunch of interior decorating magazines, and a self-help book about finding love after loss. No yearbook.

I'm halfway through tackling the Leaning Tower of Pisa when I hear the front door open. For a second there, the tower tips to the right, but I reach my hands out just in time to steady it.

"Drew?"

It's Filipe. With the worst timing possible.

"Hold on a sec," I shout. I quickly check to make sure everything is as I found it. I step back out into the hallway, leaving Mom's bedroom door slightly ajar. By the time I'm thumping down the stairs, I hear Filipe turn on the TV.

He's slumped back on my sofa. "Our AC's busted,"

he says as he kicks off his sneakers. "Want to play Crash Landing?"

"Uh, okay," I say. Any other day I would—who doesn't want to play Crash Landing? I heard that in Japan and South Korea there are special centers to help people who are addicted to the game. But right now all I want is an empty house.

Filipe shoots me a funny look. "Did I interrupt something?"

"No," I lie, settling into the sofa beside him. There's no way I'll be able to finish searching my mom's room now that Filipe's here. Still, a tiny part of me is glad he came over. Maybe hanging out with Theo was just a one-time thing, and that's why he wanted to keep it one-on-one. It's not every day that an eighth grader comes over your house to shoot hoops. I get that.

Filipe starts up the game. "So, what was the deal with that guy? Did he stay the night? I saw his bike there the next morning."

I wish I could tell him. Just spell it out, like how I did earlier today with Audrey. But I don't think I can, because then I'd have to talk about my dad, and we haven't talked about him in forever.

With Audrey, I could just talk about Phil because

she doesn't know the truth about my dad. But Filipe does. Filipe was there through all of that. My dad's not just some idea to him, he's a real person.

And Filipe knew what things were like after. Even if we don't talk about that time now, I know he remembers. I don't know how he could forget.

Plus, what if he told Theo? Never mind if I'm wrong. No, I can't tell him.

"Just some old friend of my mom's," I say.

"Not her boyfriend?" He makes his avatar, Argon28437, do the little dance he's been practicing in the waiting area.

I fake a laugh. "Nope. Just passing through town."

Suddenly the wait is over, and now Filipe's avatar is being dropped from the plane. He zooms over the island, scouting out places to land. My favorite is the forest, but Filipe always goes for the more urban areas. He deploys the parachute.

"Too bad," he says. "You could've ridden on that Harley."

Filipe's avatar is off and running, chopping down trucks and buildings to get supplies. I go into the kitchen to get us some snacks. I put some popcorn and cookies in a bowl and grab a few sodas from the fridge.

Filipe cracks open a Sprite and slurps from it.

How would it be if Phil were still here? Is he the kind of grown-up who plays video games? My dad sure wasn't. Not modern video games, at least. He was a fan of the really old-school games, like at the arcade. He could PAC-MAN like nobody's business.

But I couldn't picture him here with Filipe and me. Nestled down into the sofa, or legs spread out on the floor, playing video games long into the night like we would on weekends, or those weeknights late in the summer when Mom finally gave up on bedtimes.

I could kind of picture Phil playing with us, though. He'd probably whip up some kind of interesting snack—like super-spicy popcorn—and I bet he'd have fun exploring the island. I can't see him being into fighting people, like Filipe. Probably more into building forts and walls. Like me.

Filipe suddenly mutes the game. "What's up with you?"

"Huh?"

"You're not even paying attention. You're not begging me to explore the forest or telling me to chase down Mermaidgyrl666. It's like you're not even here."

"Sorry?" I say.

"Look, if you didn't want me to come over, you could've just said so."

"You let yourself into my house!" Of course I want him to come over—just not right now. I want to pretend that whole weird thing with Theo never happened. But I can't say that, either. I decide to change the subject. "Do you want to go to the fair next week?"

"The county fair?"

As if there's another one. We've only been going every summer for our whole lives.

Filipe scrunches his nose. "The rides there are weak. I'd rather go to Six Flags."

Before I have a chance to say Six Flags is also an hour away and not what I was inviting him to in the first place—and that maybe the rides *are* weak, but the rest of the fair is fun—the front door opens. Mom's got her arms full of groceries, and Xan's feeling the need to demonstrate his latest tae kwon do moves.

"Be careful with the coffee table!" Mom says from the kitchen, but she's a second too late. His kick just grazes the edge of the coffee table, enough to knock over my Dr Pepper. Brown liquid pools on the hardwood floor.

"I'm sorry," Xan says. "It was an accident."

"They always are, aren't they?" Mom ruffles my brother's hair.

I leap to get some paper towels to dry it up. By the time I'm back in the living room, the couch is empty. "Did Filipe leave?" I ask, setting the paper towels over the spill. I step on them, soaking up the spill real good.

"He had to head back for dinner," Mom says. "Speaking of, I could use your help in the kitchen in a minute. Thanks, bud. I'd ask Xander to clean up his own spill, but you know how well that'd go."

The floor is still sticky, so I grab some cleaning spray and go at the spill until the floor's as smooth as it was before. If only there was a way to do that with Filipe—smooth over everything. But I don't think it's that easy.

Later that night, I lie awake in bed, waiting for that *thunk* when Mom puts her book on the bedside table, the *click* of her turning off her light. It's after ten, so she should be going to sleep any minute now.

As far as she knows, I'm already asleep. My light's been off for more than half an hour. The only thing keeping me awake is the bright glow of my phone's screen, hidden under my covers. Plus the pounding of my heart as I imagine what I might find tonight.

Thunk. Click.

One thing that's always been true about my mom is how quickly she falls asleep. Dad used to give her a hard time about it because it took him forever to go to sleep, but Mom could fall asleep anywhere. Long car rides, in the dark at the movies. She used to fall asleep on Xander's bed back when he was little and needed someone in the room until he drifted off.

I wait until it's been five minutes on my phone, and then I crack open my door and tiptoe down the hallway. The door to Mom's bedroom is ajar and I can hear the tiny whistling sound her nose makes when she's conked out.

I creep down the stairs and then flick on the lights. After helping Mom with supper and cleanup, then Xander's bedtime story, there hasn't been any time to look at the books in the living room. But maybe it's better this way. Now I have all the time I need with no one interrupting me.

The place that makes the most sense to start is the big bookcase in the living room, because that's where the oldest books are. Way at the top, those cheap tiny paperbacks, in the middle the bigger paperbacks and hardcovers, and down toward the bottom, everything oversize—coffee-table books, cookbooks, magazines, old college textbooks with the yellow "used" stickers. I get down on my knees, tracing the copies with my fingers to make sure I don't miss anything.

A book about the Newport mansions, a cookbook from when Mom went through her vegetarian phase, old copies of *Gourmet* magazine. *It's got to be here somewhere.*

My fingers hit a bound white book, no words on the spine. It's thin, just the right width for a yearbook. *Please be it.* Holding my breath, I tug it out carefully, pulling out the book next to it just a bit so I know where to put it back. But when I have it out all the way, when I can see what it really is, I almost drop it.

Centered on the cover is a black-and-white photo of my mom and dad, surrounded by their friends and family with sparklers in their hands. It must be from their wedding day. I've seen some pictures before— there used to be one on the mantel of just Mom and Dad, and another in the hallway upstairs, them with all their friends and family. The photographer must've asked them all to jump, so they were all up in the air, every one of them except for Mom's roommate from college, Libby, who I guess wasn't paying attention. But I've never seen this book before. The pages are stiff. Makes sense, I guess. No one's turned these pages in years.

Inside, the pictures are in color. Photos of their wedding cake, Mom's bouquet, her dress hanging on a fancy hanger with *Mrs.* twisted into the wire, their wedding bands on top of a velvet bag.

I figured Mom got rid of all this stuff. That a book like this would be sitting in one of those boxes in the shed out back. But maybe there are some things you can't get rid of.

They look so young in the pictures, Mom and Dad. Not high school young, more like they just got out of college. That's where they met in Boston. At least, I think? Mom was in grad school to be a librarian, Dad was in dental school.

I get to the page where they're stuffing cake into each other's mouths. Mom missed by a mile, probably because she was laughing so hard. Dad's got frosting on his glasses.

He doesn't look like a person who would ever do that, what he did. He's too happy.

It would have made at least some sense if he'd been

different. If he'd been the kind of person who wanted to sleep all day. Or if he had a drinking problem, like some adults. Something. But that wasn't true.

He had everything. Everything nice he could have wanted. A nice house, a nice car, a nice job. Our life was fine three years ago. More than fine. It was great.

He stares back at me, smiling, laughing, his eyes twinkling. I can't stand to look at him for one more second. I slam the photo album shut. Chuck it across the room. It hits the sofa, barely making a noise, which I guess is good, because the last thing I want to do is wake up Mom.

I don't want you to be my dad.

I turn back to the shelf and stare at the books until my vision's not so blurry anymore. I finish that whole shelf. No yearbook. Check the shelf below it. The one above. Double-check. Triple-check. Quadruple-check.

Mom moved a lot as a kid. Maybe she didn't care about getting a yearbook because she barely knew her classmates after changing schools so many times. I guess it *could* be in her room, but now that I'm thinking about it, the bookshelves I ran out of time to check aren't the right size for something as big as a yearbook. If it wasn't on her bedside table, it's probably not there.

I check the clock to see how long I've been down here, and I have to do a double-take when I see the time. Just after midnight.

When I go to get up, one of my legs has fallen asleep. It's on pins and needles as I walk over to the couch to grab the wedding photo book. I can't help myself from flipping through it one last time.

It's the youngest I've ever seen my dad that I can remember. He doesn't look like me. His eyes, his long straight nose, his thin mouth. I don't look like him. Not really. No, not at all.

"Maybe it was never you," I whisper to that picture of him, his eyes full of love as he stares back at Mom.

After I've shoved the book back into its place, I flick off the light downstairs.

Passing by Mom's room, I peek inside. She's got her back toward me, her head facing the window. The curtains sway in a cool breeze. What does she think about Dad now? Does she still hate him sometimes? Has she forgiven him?

I crawl back under my covers. Even though it's super late, my mind's too awake to fall asleep, so I reach for my phone.

There aren't any pictures of Dad there. I didn't

get the phone until fifth grade. But there are a few pictures of him floating around online. Like the one that used to be on the website for his dental office. He's wearing a blue button-down shirt, a tie, and a blazer, and standing in front of some ivy-covered wall the photographer must have picked out. His smile is closed-mouth, which is kind of funny when you think about it. Wouldn't he want his patients to know he has nice teeth?

I stare at that picture so long it's got to be burned into my retinas.

I hate that picture because it's exactly how I remember him now. I remember that picture more than I remember the actual him. But that picture is all I have left.

And one day, one day it's not going to be there when I search for it. The website for his office is long gone. I don't even know why that picture is still find-able. Google made some kind of mistake. And some-day they're going to fix it and that last picture of Dad will be gone too. Gone forever.

THE FOLLOWING MORNING AT THE

library, Audrey's helping me get supplies ready for tomorrow's craft program when I break the news to her. "I couldn't find the yearbook."

"What about the spit?"

"I didn't look for his spit!"

A mom browsing the picture books with a baby swaddled to her chest cranes her neck, shooting me a funny look.

I lower my voice. "But I was thinking . . . you

know how upstairs we have all the yearbooks for the high school? In the local history room?"

"But he didn't grow up here."

"I know." Typical Audrey. Always assuming she's a few steps ahead of me, when actually sometimes I can be a few steps ahead of her. "But there's a way to get stuff from other libraries, right? Even faraway ones."

"Interlibrary loan!" Audrey says.

"Exactly. You in?"

"In . . . what?" Audrey asks.

"Like, do you want to help me?"

"Oh, sure." She drops the basket of scissors, scattering kid-safe scissors all over the stained carpet.

I reach down to help her pick them up, accidentally grabbing the same one she's going for. Audrey pulls her hand away fast.

"How about this afternoon?" I ask, standing up. "When the zoo guy comes?"

"Audrey?" Mrs. Eisenberg calls over. "Can you give me a hand here? The screen's freezing up again."

"I better go help Mrs. Eisenberg." Audrey sets the basket of scissors down on the table.

••••

That afternoon Mrs. Eisenberg is in the program room with a bunch of elementary school kids and a guy from the Roger Williams Zoo who comes every summer with all kinds of animals. You can always tell which day he's coming because it's the one day all summer that Mrs. Eisenberg puts on makeup. And I don't think it's to impress the kinkajou.

Right before the program, there were a bunch of kids hanging out at the coloring tables. I sent Audrey over with some new crayons, thinking that could help win them over. She was doing such a good job talking to them about their drawings that she didn't even catch me flashing her a thumbs-up from across the room.

For a second I thought I might have to save her with a cough when she started talking about Salvador Dalí and Pablo Picasso while they stared back at her blankly, but then she pulled out a save, talking about what fun colors they used.

Maybe she's not as scared of kids as she thought. (Well, so long as none of them sneeze on her.)

Down here now there's just a nanny with a baby, grabbing some board books and visiting the fish in the aquarium. Audrey is at Mrs. Eisenberg's computer organizing files, and I'm trying to figure out which book to zombify for my next story-hour puppet show. Mrs. Eisenberg pulled a whole stack of them for me earlier.

I've just finished *Creepy Carrots*—that book doesn't need to be zombified at all, it's already too frightening for most toddlers—when I hear Audrey whisper, "Drew!" from across the room.

I put *Creepy Carrots* in the "no" pile and head over to the computer.

"So I've been thinking . . ." Audrey scoots over on her chair, making room for me.

"Yeah?" I say as I squeeze in. The chair looked bigger before, and now that I'm sitting in it, I can feel my leg against Audrey's, and I wish I'd just pulled up another chair. Too late now. I try to shift my leg over the tiniest bit, but it's still kind of touching Audrey's.

"Loretta is in charge of interlibrary loans."

"Yeah."

"That's a problem."

"Why?"

"Because she shares an office with your mom. Don't you think she'll say something to your mom if you place an interlibrary loan?"

"I hadn't thought about that. . . ."

"Well, good thing you have *me* thinking about all the possibilities."

Yeah, Audrey. I just love having someone tell me to use my brain. It's the best.

I take a deep breath. It's not the first time Audrey's gotten on my nerves, and I'm sure it won't be the last. But I need her. And anyway, I already told her my secret—well, part of it. We're in this together now. "So, what should we do?"

"We're going to have to create a fake patron."

"Wait—what?"

"Someone else needs this yearbook. For a *different* reason. Actually, not just somebody else. Eliza P. Muffinbottom."

"Who the heck is that?"

Audrey clicks at the bottom of the screen, opening the library database.

"You didn't . . . ," I start to say.

But no.

She did.

The library database shows a person with library card bar code number 20572847575375. Eliza P. Muffinbottom, birth date: 3/14/1946, address: 134

Thistle Lane, Smithtown, Rhode Island 02846.

"We can delete her when we're done."

"You made a library card for a fake person?"

Audrey glares at me. I didn't say it *that* loud.

I twist my neck to see if the nanny heard us, but she's in the rocking chair reading to that baby, and she doesn't seem to have noticed.

"Not a library *card*." Audrey lowers her voice to a whisper. "Just a record."

"How are we even going to make this work? You planning to dress up as Mrs. Muffinbottom? Or is that on me?"

"No one has to dress up as her." Audrey shakes her head. "That would never work. Sheesh. Come on, Drew."

"I don't get it."

"We just need the interlibrary loan to get processed. I'll e-mail the request—"

"How?"

She clicks below, opening up a page for Gmail where, sure enough, she's set up an e-mail address: catladymuffin@gmail.com.

"You're officially insane." I stand up. "I don't think I can share a chair with you anymore."

"Come on, Drew."

"You're nuts. This will never work. I mean, even if Loretta places the hold for you with whatever crazy story you come up with, what are we going to do when it comes in? Who's going to pick it up, huh? What's next? You place an ad on Craigslist for an old lady to pretend to be her?"

"Hey, I didn't think of that. That's actually not a bad idea."

I'm shaking my head as I step away from the computer. I should've never told her. It was a mistake. She's going to find a way to ruin this. Her plan is crazy. Plus, I don't even really know her. I only met her on Monday—four days ago. Who's to say she'll keep this secret? I want to bury myself in a pile of puppets. Can't we just go back to the beginning of the summer, where all I had to worry about was enough material for the zombie story hour? Not Phil possibly being my dad or why Filipe suddenly doesn't want to hang out with me.

"Drew." Audrey's chewing on her lip.

"What?"

"Where do you think I go every day during story hour?"

"Huh?"

"Haven't you noticed I'm not in the room when you do that?"

She isn't? I guess I'm too busy telling the story to notice. Keeping the little kids happy doesn't leave much room in my mind to worry about Audrey.

"Mrs. Eisenberg has me go upstairs to help Loretta open up the interlibrary loans from out of state. Something about her getting too many paper cuts from doing it herself, I don't know."

Oh.

I sit back down. This time, I don't care so much about our legs touching. "Why didn't you say that first?"

"Why did you assume I didn't know what I was doing? I told you, Drew. I thought this all out."

"Okay, but can we make her name a little less crazy so she at least sounds like a real person?"

"Yeah. Of course. Any name you want. This was just an example."

"Just an example," I repeat under my breath. The whole thing is still a little nuts. And we could get caught. But it's not like what we're doing is so crazy. We're not planning a bank robbery or anything. Just trying to track down a high school yearbook.

"Sorry, Mrs. Muffinbottom, but I'm going to have to kill you." Audrey presses delete on her record and, poof, no more Mrs. Muffinbottom. "So." She turns to me. "Who do we want to create?"

Heavy thumps come from the stairwell. Not like little kids, though. And then the door flings open wide.

"Hey, what's he doing here?" a familiar voice asks.

It's Theo . . . and Filipe.

I LEAP UP FROM THE CHAIR, LEAVING

Audrey behind.

"I . . . I work here," I say to Theo.

Guess Filipe didn't say anything to him. What are they doing here, anyway? I don't think I've seen Filipe in the library since we were in second grade.

"Wait, really?"

Filipe heads straight for the computer area, plops down on one of the swivel chairs, and connects his phone to the computer with a small white cord. It's Theo who walks over toward us.

"Well, I don't get paid, exactly . . ."

"Then you don't really work here," Filipe says under his breath.

Jeez. What crawled up his butt? Is he still upset about me being too quiet or whatever when we were playing Crash Landing yesterday?

"That's kinda cool, though." Theo picks up one of Mrs. Eisenberg's glass paperweights and tosses it casually in the air. Like it's not completely breakable or anything. "At least this place has air-conditioning. Unlike my house."

"Heh." I manage a little laugh.

He clunks the paperweight back down on her desk right before I have a small heart attack.

"You got it working okay?" Theo walks over to Filipe.

"No. Ugh. I think it really died this time." Filipe checks the connection on the cord and his phone.

"Can I help?" Audrey asks.

Before I have a chance to say it's a terrible idea, Audrey's already jogging over there. I'm caught between following her and staying right where I am. Both of them seem like the wrong choice.

"Your phone?" she asks.

"Yeah." Filipe glances over at me, raising his eyebrows. Oh, right! I told him about Audrey. It was only a few days back, but man, it feels like forever ago. "It was working just fine, but then the screen went all black."

"Did you try a hard reboot?"

"A *what?*"

"Let me see." Audrey takes over his chair and grabs his phone, which is still plugged into the computer's USB port. "Yikes, this screen is really cracked. You know they make protective cases, right?"

"No way." Theo chuckles.

"Are you like some tech expert?" Filipe leans back in his chair, putting his feet up on the table. Where does he think he is? Back in his living room?

Audrey ignores the question. "All you have to do is press these two buttons and hold down until . . . see? Did you hear that?"

"Maybe?" Filipe shrugs.

"Hey, it's working! She fixed it." Theo raises his hand for a high five. Audrey cautiously reaches out her own palm and gives him a little tap. "That could use some work."

Audrey keeps her head down as she retreats to Mrs. Eisenberg's computer.

"So, you're gonna text Sophia? See if she wants to meet us at the park?" Theo's sitting on the computer table now, thumping the metal leg with the back of his foot.

Who's Sophia? Some eighth grader from soccer camp?

"Yeah, yeah, I said I'll do it, all right? Just . . . I need a sec. It's still booting up."

"Dude, your phone is ancient."

"I don't see you using your phone to text her. At least I didn't drop mine in the toilet for, like, the fifth time."

"It was only three times," Theo says, sliding off the table. "Jeez." He scans the wall with the chart tallying the hours the kids have read each week, the one I helped Mrs. Eisenberg make back when school let out.

"They still have these things? Like with prizes and everything?"

"You mean . . . summer reading?" I ask. "Yup." I gesture to the prize drawer.

"That stuff is junk," Filipe says, peeking at it. "I won this yo-yo, right? Thing broke the first day I brought it home. Come on, Theo. Let's go."

"See you later, Drew," Theo says.

"Later." I raise my hand to wave goodbye, but when it's halfway up, I realize how absolutely stupid and unnecessary it is and try to lower it before anyone notices.

The door has barely closed behind them when Audrey pipes up, "So, who were they?"

"My friend Filipe and Theo."

"Wait a second. *Friend*?"

"He lives across the street from me."

"Okay, that I believe. But friend? He didn't even acknowledge your existence. His friend Theo was kind of okay. Not, like, going to be winning genius awards anytime soon, but—"

"Audrey, just—can you stop? It's not like you're exactly popular."

Audrey's smile disappears in an instant. The color drains from her face and for a second, I think she's going to cry. She goes quiet, reaching up to adjust her glasses. "At least I'm new here," she spits out.

Without saying another word, she heads straight for the restroom, the door slamming shut behind her. Across the room, the nanny pokes her head up, like she's checking to make sure everything's okay.

Real nice, Drew.

It was one thing to think it, but another to actually say it to her face. Especially after how helpful she's been. I wish I could take it back. Rewind and do over the last minute. Or maybe rewind even further back, and start over again when Filipe and Theo came down here. Maybe it's impossible to make Filipe think the library is cool, but I was definitely not doing the place any favors.

Why is it that all of a sudden I can say hardly anything to Filipe? Maybe he wasn't so wrong yesterday when he called me out for being so quiet.

Across the room, the nanny is still sitting with the baby. Pointing at the pictures, showing her all the tiny details that she probably can't even understand because she's just some dumb little baby.

It was Dad who used to take Filipe and me to story hour when we were little. Mom was pregnant with Xan and she had such bad morning sickness she couldn't even work. Dad's office assistant must have known not to schedule any root canals for that hour right before lunch. We'd sit downstairs on the carpet, Filipe and me, and listen to Mrs. Eisenberg's stories before heading off to afternoon kindergarten.

Dad must've gone upstairs to browse because he'd

come back down with a big bag of books every time. Back then I couldn't believe he read so many pages—without pictures.

What would Dad think if he could see how Filipe had come down here and pretended he barely even knew me?

That's the kind of thing you're supposed to be able to talk to your dad about. If your dad didn't desert you.

I mean, Filipe. Of all people.

When I returned to school after Dad died, Filipe was the only one who treated me like I was normal. For the rest of third grade, I didn't get invited to a single birthday party. Not even one. Did they think they were going to catch something from me? That suicide was contagious? The only one who didn't back away was Filipe.

Until now. Maybe now that we're older, Filipe's having some of the same questions I am. Worrying that maybe I *am* like Dad, or I could be. If he is my real dad, I mean. That someday I could do what he did. Maybe that's why he's keeping his distance. Maybe that's what he was trying to say about me being too quiet.

Suddenly I hear a stampede of footsteps coming

down the stairs. The zoo program must have ended and the kids are as amped as ever. I close all the windows Audrey left open on Mrs. Eisenberg's computer and head over to the tables, already set up for this afternoon's craft: paper-chain snakes with googly eyes.

I'm helping Mrs. Eisenberg get the kids settled when the door to the women's restroom finally opens. Audrey's face isn't red, but for how long she's been in there, she must have been crying. I want to apologize, but she won't even make eye contact with me. She beelines for Mrs. Eisenberg's computer and immediately pops in her earbuds.

Were we really just moments away from creating a believable fake-sounding person and requesting the yearbook? So much for that.

19

"COME ON." XANDER WHIPS THE

sheet off me the next morning, breathing warm maple syrup breath all over my face. "Come on, Doodoo. Mom says we can go to the beach today."

"I told you a billion times, I won't be seen with you in public if you call me that."

When he was just learning to talk, Xan struggled with my name. He couldn't get his *R*s out right, so he called me Doo, and then Doodoo.

"Fine!" he huffs, standing at the foot of my bed, waiting for me to get up.

I should want to. It's the beach, after all. Swimming until your arms ache (or you've swallowed too much salt water, whichever comes first). Lying in the warm sun. Watching Xan chase seagulls and fail to catch them. There's no such thing as a *bad* day at the beach.

But after how things ended yesterday, all I want is to skip over the weekend and fast-forward to Monday. After coming out of the bathroom, Audrey didn't talk to me for the rest of the day. I know I deserved it, but still.

"Okay, okay." I jump out of bed and run over to tickle my brother.

"Stop, stop!" Xan pants in between giggling fits.

"You know I'll do it again if you ever call me—"

"I won't! I won't! Promise! Cross my fart."

I release him, and he zooms out of my bedroom, giggling, his tiny feet thumping the hardwood stairs. I flip open my front shade and stare across the street at Filipe's house. Last summer I would have texted him at the first mention of the beach. But between how he acted when I tried to play basketball with him and Theo and how annoyed he got at me during Crash Landing the other day—never mind the library—I don't know what to do anymore to make things go back to normal.

If I don't exist to him, maybe . . . maybe he shouldn't exist to me either.

I grab my phone off the bedside table and check to see if there are any messages. Nope. I toss it back on my bed and dig around in my dresser for my bathing suit.

It's Saturday, after all.

"Oh, come on. Another fire hydrant! You've got to be kidding me." Mom groans.

"Sorry," I say. "That one came out of nowhere."

As we inch down the road leading to the beach in Westerly, I crane my neck, searching for an empty parking spot or someone backing out of theirs. We've made two loops already and still nothing.

"I see one!" Xan yells. He points out his window, half-open to let in the salty air. There's nothing like the smell of the ocean—nothing.

"No way," I say. But sure enough, on the other side of the street is a woman maneuvering her black MINI Cooper out of the world's tiniest parking spot.

"That's going to be a tight squeeze," Mom says.

"You can totally do it. Want me to hop out?"

Mom doesn't look very certain. "If you really think so."

I get out and direct our car into the spot. Sure, it might be a five-million-point turn. And we might be three centimeters from touching the bumper of the car behind us. But, technically, we're in.

"Don't know what I'd do without you." Mom pops the trunk to get our beach towels and the cooler. "My navigator." She ruffles my hair.

I squeeze a dollop of sunscreen for my face, and then I grab my brother's hand while we half walk, half jog down the street. Xan likes to run ahead of Mom, which means I have to chase after him. Once he gets a view of the beach and the carousel, there's not much that can slow him down.

The beach can get crowded on summer weekends, but if you get here early enough, like us, you can still snag a good spot. We lay our beach blanket a few yards from the lifeguard tower. Mom tries to get Xan to put on sunscreen before dashing into the sea, but like usual, he makes a big fuss about it.

I dart after him as he kicks up sand. "Hey, watch out for other people's blankets," I remind him. The sun makes me squint, even in my sunglasses.

The funny thing about my brother is, no matter how excited he is about the beach, every time he reaches the water, he slows down. There's something about the ocean. How tremendous it is . . . and how you can't control it. Xan respects that. I know I do.

Xan stays in the shallow water, jumping over the small waves as they crash into the shore and picking up particularly grody pieces of seaweed. Mom makes her way toward him, haloed by the sun.

Once she has her eye on him, I wade in deeper until I'm up to my chest, and then I let the water just hold me as I float on my back.

Down the way a bit are two teenage girls in bikinis, splashing each other. One is mad that the other messed up her hair.

Has Audrey been to the beach yet in Rhode Island?

I can't imagine her here. For one, she's exactly the type of person who'd get squeamish if one bit of seaweed clung to her arm. Or worse, if she got some sand in her bathing suit. And she definitely has the kind of skin that'll burn lobster red if she isn't careful with sunscreen.

Wait.

I'm not even at the library. Why in the heck am I thinking about *Audrey*?

I swim out a bit farther, watching as a yacht cruises by in the distance, until I'm so far out I can barely see my mom. She doesn't need to worry. The whole reason we come to Watch Hill instead of Misquamicut in the first place is because the waves are so tame here. No undertow at all.

Last summer Filipe made fun of us for still coming here. Called it the kiddie beach. He said all the high schoolers went to Misquamicut, and now that we were in middle school, we needed to go there too.

Whatever.

Maybe it's better here without him. I don't need someone telling me what's cool and what isn't every five seconds.

I tread water for a while, watching as a seagull by the shore dive-bombs the blanket of someone who left their food unattended. A woman runs out from the water, yelling and waving to get the seagull out of her stuff. I hope someone's recording this for YouTube.

One time when I was little, after a long day at the beach, I asked my dad if I could have a seagull as a pet. I guess somehow I'd convinced myself that a seagull was a beautiful bird, like a penguin or a peacock or something. It happens when you're little—you think you're really onto something, except no one else agrees with you. Dad had laughed at me. Not an odd reaction; I'm sure he couldn't help it in the moment, but I guess it'd been a long day and I was tired and hungry and I just—I lost it. I cried and cried about it the whole way home.

And then a few mornings later, when I woke up, there was a new stuffed animal nestled in my arms. I don't know where my dad found a stuffed seagull, but he had.

I'd forgotten about that day until just now. Most of the things I remember from being a little kid, they're not because I really remember them. They're because we still talk about them. That's what keeps them alive. The story of what happened replaces the memory. Or maybe the story strengthens it.

If you don't talk about things, eventually you forget them. Completely.

I stay in the water a long time, only coming out because my fingertips are raisin-y and my stomach is growling. Back by our blanket, Xan and Mom are hard at work on a sandcastle. Xan slopped a bunch of seaweed onto the turrets, giving the castle kind of a creepy Hogwarts vibe.

I help myself to one of the wraps we grabbed at the deli and sit in a beach chair. Sand sticks to the back of my wet legs as I bite into the crunchy lettuce and tuna.

"What was Filipe up to today?" Mom asks. "Were they heading out of town for the weekend?"

I pretend my mouth is full.

"Everything okay with you two? He left kind of quickly the other day." She raises her voice. "Xan, watch out, honey, you're getting sand all over the blanket."

"I don't know," I say with a shrug. There's no way I can talk to Mom about how Filipe's been lately. She'd never understand.

Mom sweeps off the sand my brother got all over the blanket. I scarf down the rest of my sandwich, and then get on my hands and knees, helping Xan and Mom with the sandcastle.

After more swimming and napping, the beach starts to clear out again. Families head home for supper while we're putting the finishing touches on the grandest sandcastle of the day. Xan carefully sticks a seagull feather into the top of the tallest turret.

Somehow the bridge over the moat is still holding strong, though I know it's only a matter of time before the water takes down the whole thing. The tide is coming in, and in another hour it'll take out our sandcastle. Wipe it all away, like it never even existed.

After we pack up all our stuff, there's just one thing left to do.

Mom heads into the changing rooms to switch out of her wet swimsuit and into dry clothes for the ride home while I wait with Xan by the carousel, watching the painted horses go around and around and around. It's tradition. You can't visit Watch Hill and not stop at the carousel. It's more than a hundred years old, one of the oldest in the whole country.

The sunburned teenage girl working the ride keeps checking her watch, like she can't wait for her shift to be over so she can do something more exciting. I hand her the money for one ride and then Xan runs straight for his favorite horse. Tan and spotted, with a long blond mane and a red saddle. I help him up, get him all buckled in, and head back outside the gate to watch.

As the music starts, the carousel slowly whirs to life. It never goes real fast—it's a carousel, after all, not a roller coaster—but it's fast enough that you have to practice your timing to get a ring. About halfway through the ride, they sling out this machine with rings for everyone to reach out and grab. There are a few special golden rings mixed in with all the silver ones, and if you're lucky enough to get one of those, you earn a free ride.

Xan rounds the corner, grinning and holding up a ring to show me he's gotten it. Last year his arms weren't quite long enough to reach.

Next thing I know, Mom is standing next to me.

"He got a ring," I tell her.

She wraps her arm around me. "I saw! God, we'll never hear the end of it if he gets a gold one."

"Probably not. Wait—what if he *keeps* getting the gold one? What if he's stuck riding the carousel forever?"

Mom laughs. "That sounds like a horror movie."

The carousel keeps turning around and around. On the bookshelf in our living room, there's a framed photo of me that time I got the gold ring. Dad must've taken it; he took most of the photos with that big fancy camera of his.

Is it weird that it feels almost normal now? Just the three of us? I should feel like someone's missing. Like there's a big gaping hole in our family.

I should, but a lot of the time I don't.

I stare at the carousel, the past flaking away like the paint on the hundred-year-old horses. What if it was never supposed to be Dad taking me to the beach all those times? What if it should've been Phil? But wait. If I'm really Phil's son, why would he wait so long to be a part of my life, anyway? Would he really just let Dad raise me? Was that *why* Dad did it? Because he couldn't stand living a lie? The questions—the possibilities—start branching out again. Maybe they're not like a tree at all, but a web. A big, tangled web.

"Drew?"

"Yeah?" I stammer.

"Everything okay, bud?"

I nod. "Yeah. Fine."

"You were staring off into space for a while there." Mom squeezes my shoulder. "Look who got the gold ring!"

My brother whirs by, a beaming smile on his face. One more ride.

I know what I have to do on Monday. I have to fix things with Audrey. We need to get our hands on that yearbook. Until Phil gets back into town, it's all we have, and I need to know.

If there's a chance—a real chance—he's actually my dad, I need to do something about it before he leaves again—this time, for good.

IT'S NOT EASY TO TELL A PERSON

like Audrey that you're sorry. For starters, she's got a pretty intense resting face. Her stare could bore holes in the wall.

It's not until halfway through Monday morning, when I'm putting away the puppets after story hour, that I work up the courage to even say hi to her and see where we stand.

Did being apart for the weekend maybe . . . help?

Mrs. Eisenberg is across the room recommending books for a fourth grader. Now's my chance.

wasn't my *real* dad? Does it undo everything that hap pened? My whole life?

I don't think I can tell. Not yet, anyway. There's so much I won't know until I *know*, for sure, who Phil really is to me.

Audrey beckons me toward her, and I come.

"When can we do it?" she asks.

I think through today's schedule. "After lunch?"

Mrs. Eisenberg usually lets me and Audrey go to lunch first. She likes to take a later lunch, leaving us alone downstairs for about half an hour. It's the quietest time of the day. As she always tells us, if anyone comes in and needs help, the librarians upstairs are just a phone call away.

"Okay," Audrey says. "After lunch it is."

I glance at the clock. "An hour and a half to think of a better name than Mrs. Muffinbottom."

Audrey grins. "You're on."

I'm sitting at the table cutting out star name tags for tomorrow's story hour. Audrey's at Mrs. Eisenberg's computer.

The Devlin twins are taking *forever* choosing summer reading prizes. I can practically hear Mrs.

Audrey doesn't have her earbuds in as she sits at Mrs. Eisenberg's computer.

"How was your . . . weekend?"

Audrey doesn't even turn in my direction. She's got her eyes fixed on the computer screen, staring so intently she's not even blinking.

"Audrey?"

She startles and turns toward me. "Were you talking to me?"

"Um . . . yeah? I was asking . . . I mean . . . I just . . ."

Audrey stares back at me. It turns out her eyes do remember how to blink. Were they so blue like that last week? Have her eyelashes always been that long? Or did she change her glasses? Since when do I have such a hard time putting together a complete sentence around Audrey?

"You know, since I have no friends . . ."

"Audrey, I didn't mean that. Of course that's not true." Though actually, now that I think about it, for someone who just moved across the country, she doesn't seem to be texting with her old friends like you'd expect.

"What if it were true?"

"It's not," I say. "What are you even talking about?

I thought we were . . ." Why is it so hard to say? "I thought *we* were friends," I finally spit out. Why is it that I'm expecting her to laugh in my face for thinking we could be friends? "I mean—*are*."

Audrey turns back to the screen and clicks on something.

I don't understand this girl. Maybe I need to do something to show her that we're friends. Like invite her somewhere. The county fair!

"Would you want to come to the county fair with us? We usually take—" I cut myself off before saying his name. Even though what I was about to say was true, no one likes to feel like a backup choice. And anyway, Audrey's not only my friend because things have been weird with Filipe the past week.

"It's really fun," I continue. "There's rides and all kinds of good food and animals. They have cows that are ready to give birth and you can watch and everything."

Audrey swivels back around, her nose wrinkled. "Gee, Drew. You're really selling it. Cow births?" She cracks a smile. "When are you going?"

"Friday night," I say. It sounds like a date. Which it is *not*.

"Okay."

"Okay as in thumbs-up to cow birth?"

Audrey laughs. "No. Well, maybe? Okay as in it sounds fun. I've never been to a county fair before. It sounds like . . . a unique cultural experience." Leave it to Audrey to see it that way. "I'll check with my parents. Let you know tomorrow?"

"Yeah, sure."

Audrey turns back to the computer and starts typing. I'm about to head back to the tables and clean up the mess of picture books when Audrey whips around in the swivel chair once more. "Do you still want to do it, then?" Her eyes shoot across the room to Mrs. Eisenberg. That fourth grader's got quite a stack of books going, but they don't seem done.

"Get the yearbook?"

Audrey nods.

"I do," I say. More than anything. There are things I can't tell anyone. Not Audrey. Not Xan, not Mom. Not Filipe, even before this summer.

Like how I thought about him all weekend. Not Phil this time. *Dad*. I do it sometimes. Flip back through memories like they're pages in a book I've reread a million times. What would it mean if

Eisenberg's stomach rumbling at this point. She should have gone to lunch ten minutes ago, but just as she was about to leave, the two Devlin boys came racing down the stairs, trailed by their mom. They'd been out of town last week for a vacation and you would think they've been gone a whole year given how much Mrs. Devlin needs to get caught up with Mrs. Eisenberg.

Plus, it means the boys missed out on last week's summer reading prizes, and they are the most indecisive kids ever. I swear I spent half an hour helping Timmy decide which colored bouncy ball he wanted last year. I could practically feel my hair growing.

"What do you think, Timmy? How about the train whistle?" Mrs. Eisenberg reaches into the prize drawer and shows him a wooden train whistle.

Timmy grabs it from her, carefully examining it like he's never seen one before. Not possible! We went through this whole routine last summer.

"I don't know," he says.

Audrey swivels around in her chair and catches my eye.

I glance up at the clock, trying to communicate to her without words that we're in a serious time crunch. If Mrs. Eisenberg doesn't leave for lunch soon, she's going to be sneaking bites from her desk later. We've got "Reading with Dogs" starting at one p.m., and I know we're going to get a crowd for that. Who doesn't love reading to dogs from the shelter?

"You should take the train whistle," I say, getting up from the table. "It's the coolest thing ever."

Mrs. Eisenberg beams at me. "Well, if Drew thinks it's cool, you know what that means."

Timmy hugs it to his chest. "Okay. The train whistle." He presses his mouth to it and blows hard. No returning it now.

Even his mom looks relieved. "Let's go home for lunch, boys."

Timmy's twin brother, Daniel, gets up from the table where he's been coloring. "Finally!"

Mrs. Eisenberg's too polite to say what we've all been thinking in front of the Devlins, but when the door closes behind them, she lets out a sigh and grabs a spoon from her desk drawer. "Got to beat the dogs," she says, heading for the elevator. "You know how to reach me."

"Yup." I head back over to the table like I'm about to cut some more name tags, but once the elevator door closes behind Mrs. Eisenberg, I'm darting across the room, rolling over a free chair to squeeze in beside Audrey.

She's got the screens open already.

"This is going to be tight," she says, and I can feel my heart hammer. "But I'm prepared." She opens up a Word document. It's got to have a hundred names on it.

"When did you—"

"Eh, I got started over the weekend. And then I kept adding to it when a new one came to me."

Over the weekend. So was she just faking being mad at me?

She scrolls down the list. "Which one do you like best, or—do you have one?"

"I had a couple," I say, though none of them compare to this. The amount of time that went into this. Just, wow. "That one," I say, pointing to a good one. *John Jacob Langham.*

"Not this one?" Audrey highlights *Ethel Finkelstinkle.*

"Yeah, no." I laugh. "I mean, you can make a fake library account for her if you really want to, but let's request the yearbook under a normal-sounding name."

Audrey creates a library account for John Jacob Langham, along with a fake street address in town, and a fake e-mail address, too. She comes up with an elaborate backstory for why he needs the yearbook—he lost his in a house fire—and then she hits send. We stare at the Gmail screen, waiting for a response from Loretta. Suddenly I smell coconut and pineapple.

How'd I get so close to Audrey that I can smell her hair? I creep my chair away until I'm at a more appropriate distance.

"So." Audrey swivels her chair so she's facing me. "I held a baby yesterday."

"No way!" It was one thing to see her talk more with the little kids last week, but there's a big gap between little kids and an actual baby.

"My next-door neighbor came back from the hospital a few days ago and my mom asked me to go over with her to bring a gift. It all happened so fast. I said yes. And then I sort of wished I'd said no, because, you know, babies. But I went anyway and she let me hold her! This teeny-tiny baby, Drew. She couldn't really do anything at all yet, just kind of flailed around and made weird noises. Totally helpless, you know?"

"Did she spit up?"

"Yeah. A little. But not on me. Thank God."

I laugh, and Audrey does too.

"I guess I get it now, why people like babies so

much. They're just so . . . new. And innocent. And good. They haven't made any huge mistakes yet."

"Yeah," I say. I hadn't thought about it that way, but she's right. I wonder when everything changes, when suddenly your mistakes aren't the easy-to-fix kinds.

The screen saver pops up on the monitor. Audrey jiggles the mouse to wake it up, but nothing's changed. Still no new e-mails.

"What if she doesn't write ba—"

But before I've finished saying it, a new e-mail pops up.

> *Thanks for your e-mail, John. I'd be more than happy to track down a copy of your yearbook. So sorry to hear about your house. I'll get back to you once I've finalized the request.*

I can feel the tips of my ears begin to burn. Like the house that never burned down in town. Won't she wonder? A house burning down in our town—that kind of thing would be on the news.

"Why'd you write that his house burned down?" I ask.

"Because it made a good story?"

"Yeah. It does. But Loretta lives in town too. Houses don't burn down every day. What if she asks questions? What if she looks it up?"

"Relax," Audrey says. "She gets these requests all the time. She doesn't have time to think about why she gets each one. She's got work to do, you know?"

I spin around in my chair. "Maybe."

"It'll work. Trust me."

I stop spinning and stare back at Audrey.

"We'll get to the bottom of this." She wipes off her glasses on her shirt. "I can feel it."

IT'S TUESDAY AFTERNOON. AUDREY'S

on Mrs. Eisenberg's computer and I'm putting away the puppets in the craft closet when Audrey clears her throat. She clears it again. Okay, she starts legitimately hacking up a lung, and finally Mrs. Eisenberg says, "You need some water, dear?" and I look up and Audrey is glaring at me.

Oh.

Oh.

Her eyes dart to the monitor.

You know how little kids do that dance when they

have to pee and you're like, just go pee already, but they say they don't have to? And you're like, no, seriously, you do, why are you arguing with me, three-year-old despot? It's sort of like that, except I'm the kid who's so antsy I'm practically dancing as I wait, wait, wait for Mrs. Eisenberg to go somewhere—a meeting, the bathroom—or help a patron, but instead it's the quietest time in the history of the universe and she's just sitting there, feet from Audrey, checking in some new books, and I feel like I might actually explode. Not with pee, though.

Finally she gets up to use the restroom and I book it for Audrey at the computer.

"Next week!" She pulls up the e-mail from Loretta.

Well, John, you're in luck! They're sending over a copy of the 1995 yearbook and we should receive it sometime early next week. Would you like a phone call or an e-mail when it comes in?

"You wrote back 'e-mail,' right?"

"No, I figured it would be more fun to track down some guy to pretend to be John and get a cell phone with this number and—of course, silly."

"Okay. Okay. Phew."

"Back when I graduated fifth grade in Chicago, my school made yearbooks, and we got to write class wills. Maybe Phil's yearbook will have class wills! I wonder who he left things to."

I hadn't thought of that. Did he leave things to my mom? What else is even in yearbooks, anyway? Were they like Facebook before, well, Facebook?

"Guess we'll find out," I say, glancing at the e-mail again. It's coming. The yearbook will actually be here, in my—our—hands. Monday. Tuesday? Anything past that is midweek, right? So. Early next week, I'll know. Well, maybe not for sure. But I'll have enough—enough to go on to ask my mom or Phil if it's true. Mom didn't say exactly when Phil would swing back through town, but it can't be before then. He was meeting up with folks all the way in northern Maine.

"Hey, Drew?"

"Yeah?"

Audrey spins around to face me. "Are you okay with all this? Are you excited or scared or . . . ?"

"Both," I say. "I just want to know the truth. Rip off the Band-Aid already, you know?"

Audrey grimaces. "That's kind of gross."

"Depends what's under the Band-Aid. Healed scab or gushing blood."

"Okay, even grosser. I just had lunch!"

"Sorry."

"Drew?"

"Yeah."

"You want your dad to be your dad, right?"

Suddenly it's hard to look her in the eye. She doesn't know the truth about my dad. Maybe if she did, she'd get that I have so many reasons to want Phil to be my father.

"Yeah," I say to the computer monitor. "Of course."

We're both quiet for a little while, and then Audrey says, "Mrs. Eisenberg's not going to be in the bathroom forever."

"Sure. Right. Yeah. Okay." I catch Audrey eyeing me as I roll my chair back to where it's supposed to be. Her brow is furrowed and for a second I wonder if she's figured me out. She's going to find out the truth eventually. She's too smart not to.

My stomach sinks for a second. What if she gets mad at me for not telling her the truth about my dad from the start? I should have told her, or at least not made up lies on the spot. Not let her think my parents were divorced or separated. But it's too late now.

Audrey pivots and almost catches me staring at her, but I look the other way just in time. She turns back to the computer and logs out of fake John Jacob Langham's e-mail account.

My whole body feels like it's slowed down. That fake having-to-pee energy is gone, and I just feel—tired? Like I'm ready to go home. Like all I want right now is to be alone.

There's only a half hour till Mom is done for today. We're leaving early so she can take Xan to the doctor—his left ear's been hurting him and she's worried he might have an ear infection.

I head back over to the closet just as Mrs. Eisenberg is coming out of the bathroom. "Everything okay, Drew?"

"Yeah."

"You know, Mrs. Gupta was raving about your latest story. Dhipthi's evidently been doing impressions all week. A little zombie mouse constantly begging for brain cookies."

"That's . . . cool."

"You're making quite an impression on these kids. I think you could have a future in entertainment. The high school has an outstanding theater program."

"Wait, you think I can act?"

"Don't look so shocked." Mrs. Eisenberg rests a hand on her hip. "You can command a stage—if you want to, of course. Where you take your gift is up to you."

"Okay," I say, staring at my feet.

"Well, I'll let you finish up. You're doing a great job, Drew. I feel fortunate for how this whole arrangement has worked out. You've really blossomed here."

"Uh, thanks," I say as she heads back to her desk and I finally enter the closet. *Well, that was awkward.*

By the time I'm done putting the puppets away and clearing up the mess some first graders made with the puzzles, it's time to meet my mom upstairs.

It's only when I get into the stairwell, when I'm truly alone again, that I remember what happened right before Mrs. Eisenberg told me I was a flower. The yearbook. It's really coming. *Early next week.*

"You sure you don't want to come to the doctor's?" Mom sticks her head out the car window, offering like it's some kind of treat, even though we both know it isn't. Maybe she wants some company? My brother's ear appointment is in fifteen minutes.

"Doctors' offices are gross," I say. "Plus . . . I can mow the lawn while you're gone."

"Mow the lawn? You don't say! Okay, bud. See you later." Mom rolls up the car window and backs out of the driveway.

The lawn doesn't exactly need mowing yet—Phil must have lowered the setting when he mowed—but it can't hurt, either. Anything's better than hanging out in the waiting area at the doctor's with those gross piles of wrinkled old magazines. Bad paintings. Stained carpet. Weird smells.

Dad's dental office wasn't like that. He said there was no reason for a waiting room to be so sad—no wonder people dreaded seeing their doctor or the dentist! Dad's waiting room had hardwood floors, cool retro movie posters that we picked out together, and a pinball machine. Okay, so he did have a lot of random things with teeth on them, but otherwise it was possible to forget you were waiting to see the dentist.

I wish Mom had saved the pinball machine, but it was one of the first things she sold on Craigslist when she packed up his office.

I pull the mower out of the garage and check to see if it needs gas. Phil seems like the kind of guy who might use up somebody's gas and forget to say anything about it, but I check and it's full. I roll it onto the grass and rev it up, letting the whirring motor quiet my thoughts.

Clean lines across the yard. Across. Pivot. Back. Pivot. Across.

Every time a car passes up the road, I jerk my head, worried somehow it's him on his motorcycle. The yearbook has to beat him. Or come while he's here. I guess that would be okay, assuming he stays a couple days again.

But what if it doesn't? What if the post office fails and I still have no idea what's going on when he comes? What if he heads all the way back to Colorado before I know the truth?

Something catches the corner of my vision. A blur of white T-shirt and green shorts. Is Filipe really coming over after what happened at the library? He didn't come by all weekend, which, as far back as I can remember, has never happened, except for when his family's gone out of town. But I saw both his parents' cars in the driveway this weekend, so I know they were around.

He stands off to the side of my path, his mouth

moving, but I can't hear a thing over the mower.

"I can't lip-read!" I shout back at him, though he probably can't hear me either.

I finish the pass I was making and shut off the lawn mower. "What?" I ask him.

There are blue marks on either side of his lips like parentheses. Gatorade? "I was coming over to see if you wanted to bike over to the park. But, look, if you're going to be in a mood again, then never mind."

A *mood*?

"Why don't you just go with Theo? Or did he finally get sick of you? Or wait, what's her name . . . Sophia? Who even is that? Tell me you don't seriously think eighth-grade girls are going to be interested in you now."

"Sophia Carlson. She's not even an eighth grader. She lives in East Providence. We met her at camp the other week. Jeez. What's your deal?" He scratches at the edge of his mouth.

"My deal?"

"Yeah. Why were you all weird at the library?" Right. Like *I* was the one acting all weird at the library. "Did we interrupt something? You and that girl?" Filipe raises his eyebrows.

"Audrey? No!"

"Hey, you're the one who said she was some loser out to ruin your summer. But you didn't exactly seem to be having the worst time with her. Wait, do you . . . *like* her?"

"No," I spit back at him. "She's . . ."

"What?"

My friend? No, that's the last thing I can admit to Filipe. "Nothing."

Filipe tips his head back. "Oh my gosh. You *do*. You *like* her. You *like* her, like her. You totally do." He's cracking up, his eyes squinting closed, and I—I reach out and shove him. Hard. He trips on himself, catching his balance right before he hits the ground.

And then I'm on the ground on top of him, like we're play wrestling, except this time I'm not playing around. This time is for real. My hand balled into a fist, whaling and whaling on him until strong hands clasp my shoulder, wrenching us apart.

I whip around, thinking it's Phil. That somehow he's back. But it's only Anibal, all six feet of him looming over us. "What the heck?" he says.

Next to me, still on the ground, Filipe adjusts his T-shirt. Even though it felt like I was going at him hard, he doesn't seem hurt at all. Unlike my hand. I swear I can already see a bruise forming beneath the skin.

"Ask him!" Filipe points a finger at me, looking up at his brother. "We were just talking and then out of nowhere, he went all crazy on me, like . . ."

He doesn't have to say the words out loud. I hear them in my head, loud and clear. *Like his dad.*

"Well, whatever. You guys need to work this out. But Mom sent me over because she needs you, Flip."

Filipe pushes himself up to standing and brushes off grass clippings. "I was just kidding," he says under his breath. "You didn't have to go all psycho on me."

I'm still down on the ground, trying not to let Filipe see me wince as I rub my knuckles. He and Anibal exchange a few words as they wait to cross the street, but they're already out of earshot. Is Filipe telling him about Audrey, about what happened at the library the other day? Or are they both talking about Dad? Like father, like son.

They finally cross the street and disappear behind the bushes, out of sight. My knees are smeared in green from the freshly mown grass. I rub at them, but that doesn't help and only makes my palms green too.

My first fight and it's with my best friend—*former* best friend. Why did I even do it? I hate how fast it happened. One minute Filipe was picking on me, not that much more than any other time, and the next— *boom*. Something was different—had to be, because I snapped. I wasn't in control of my own body. Was that what had happened with Dad? Did something inside him just snap one day?

I hate even having to think these things. Filipe never does. He never has to worry that one day he's going to turn into his dad. That one day he could be a danger to himself. No, he's never once had that thought flit through his mind. There's no worst-case scenario in turning out just like Mr. Nunes.

I need that yearbook to come. I need to know so badly, I think maybe I am losing my mind. I can't turn into Dad. I just—I can't.

Filipe doesn't get it at all, what it's like to be me. Except sometimes, it feels like he has to. He must. Because he's so good at pressing my buttons. Picking and picking at me. Like he wants to set me off. Does he know the guilt I feel now too? That urge to text him and apologize, even if he's the one who started it?

I check my phone, start to text something to him,

but then I stop and delete it. My breath quiets down to normal as I stare at my phone for several minutes, and then I fire the lawn mower back up. This time, the whirring doesn't drown out all my thoughts. Doesn't even come close. My fingers vibrate with the motor, my whole body whirring in tune, like I'm part of the machine.

I want to do it now more than ever. Shake it all out, just like Phil. I get why he does it. Why it feels good. Letting loose all the sadness, the frustration, confusion, all the things you can't go back and fix. The fear. The hope. Except I don't want to do it so quietly. I want to shake everything out and scream at the top of my lungs.

Maybe then, some stillness would come.

FOR THE REST OF THE WEEK, FILIPE

stays clear of my house. Wednesday night, Julia comes over and she and Mom set up an outdoor movie theater in our backyard, hanging a sheet between two trees and using Julia's projector to screen *Jaws*. Turns out *Jaws* is way too scary for Xan, though, which I learn when he comes into my bed at two in the morning because of nightmares.

Also turns out sharing a bed with a wiggly six-and-a-quarter-year-old is its own kind of nightmare, and by the time I get back from the library on Thursday,

I'm practically falling asleep on the ride home. I'm so sleepy I forget to even look across the street to see if Filipe's out there playing ball.

It's not until Friday, as we're pulling out of our driveway, ready to pick up Audrey on the way over to the county fair, that I see Filipe. And even then, it's just a flash of him as he gets into Anibal's car.

It's funny—Mom didn't even ask why I didn't invite him to the fair this year. She was too busy being excited that I'd invited Audrey.

Not long after we pick up Audrey from her house, Mom turns down the radio. "Hey, Drew, Xan? Before I forget, I wanted to let you know that I've been in touch with Phil and it looks like he's about finished with the New England leg of the trip. Probably coming in late tomorrow night or Sunday morning. If it's all right with you, he'd like to stay with us again for a few days before heading back to Colorado. What do you think?"

"Yes!" Xan pumps his fist. "Motorcycle time!"

"Drew?"

Audrey squeezes my hand, startling me. But she lets go quick. "Sounds okay to me," I say, trying as hard as possible to contain my excitement. He'll be here so soon—that's a good thing. But it also means he'll be leaving so soon. Unless what we find in the yearbook changes everything.

Mom turns the radio back up, but for the rest of the ride to the fair, it's hard to concentrate. Thankfully, Xan is pretty good at one-way conversations. And he never met Audrey before, so he's plenty happy to quiz her on everything.

When we get to the fair, even though it's Audrey and not Filipe this year, Mom still feels the need to go over the ground rules. Basically, if you spend all your money on rides and games, don't come crawling back to her for money for food. A rule she had to institute after that time two years ago when Filipe really wanted to win a huge stuffed pickle with a sombrero, and used up *all* his spending money, and even then failed to win it.

Once we've passed through the turnstiles and split from Mom and Xan, I basically explode. "Tomorrow night!"

"It's so soon," Audrey says.

"What if the yearbook doesn't get here in time?" It's a thought I don't even want to think, but it's hard not to. It should be here early in the week, so as long as

Phil stays a couple days, we should be in the clear. Still.

"Maybe you should save some of his spit as a backup."

"How would I even do that?"

Audrey twists her mouth for a second. "Snag a used napkin? Wait, that'll only have food residue. A hair from his pillow, then? Is he hairy? Most men are. I'm sure there'll be a hair somewhere."

"He *is* hairy," I say.

"Well, then, there you go."

It helps to have a backup plan just in case. Not that I exactly have the money for a DNA test. I take a deep breath. *One thing at a time, Drew.* The smells of all the fair food mix together—fried dough and french fries and roast beef and clam chowder—and my nerves turn to excitement. We're going to find out. We are. It's just a matter of time.

Audrey pipes up, "I'm hungry."

Clearly all the delicious food smells are having an effect on her, too. We haven't even reached the booth where you get tickets for the rides yet. Usually Filipe and I would use up our first string of ride tickets, then get food, then go back for more rides, and then repeat until we ran out of money or it was time to go home.

"Are you sure you want to eat before we go on rides?"

Audrey stops in her tracks. "Do we *have* to go on rides?"

I stop with her. I can't remember a time I came to the county fair and *didn't* go on rides. But I also can't remember a time I came to the county fair and didn't have a stomachache half the time. Not from the food—well, maybe a little from the food—but mostly from the rides. Filipe thought it was hilarious to go on rides until he threw up.

Maybe it was the first time, but after that it was pretty gross.

"We don't have to go on rides," I tell her, suddenly relieved. If Audrey changes her mind and decides she wants to watch a cow give birth, I have a feeling it'll be a whole lot more pleasant to watch if we aren't already nauseous.

"Okay. Phew," Audrey says. "I have motion sickness. Especially with the spinning."

"Me. Too." It feels good to be able to admit the truth to her, to not have to pretend the way I have been lately with Filipe.

"So what's good to eat if I want the authentic cultural experience of the county fair? Do they have deep-fried Twinkies?"

The county fair in Rhode Island isn't exactly like state fairs I've heard about in the Midwest, where the food is as fried and weird as possible. A lot of the food booths are run by local churches and clubs—at least, the best ones are.

But Audrey doesn't know that. And it's too fun to mess with her.

"Actually, my mom was just telling me about the new snack they're debuting this year. Everyone's been talking about it. Said it was the best fair food they've ever had."

Audrey's eyes widen. "What is it? Where is it? Oh, I want to try!"

"They put it on a stick, I think. Oh man. What was it called . . . oh right! Chocolate-covered opossum. The roadkill special."

Audrey swats at me. I take a few steps back from her, not sure if there's more where that came from or not. I'm laughing, though. It was so worth it.

"They're *not* serving *that* at the fair."

"No, probably not. Let's walk around and see what looks good. Whatever's got the longest line is usually the best."

As we walk down the aisles, Audrey suddenly goes

quiet. Hopefully she's not still annoyed with me and is just scoping out the options. Lobster rolls. Spanakopita. Roast beef sandwiches. Apple crisp. There's the longest line ever at Frank's French Fries. I mean, they're pretty good french fries and they do come in a bucket, but are they worth waiting in a line for twenty minutes?

"Hey." Audrey jabs my shoulder. "Someone's calling for you." She points over to the Portuguese American Club booth. Filipe's vovó has her head stuck way out the window as she waves at me. "Who is that?" Audrey asks.

Suddenly I don't feel so hungry anymore. "Filipe's grandma."

"I bet they have good food." Audrey sniffs the air. "Smells like pork. Mmm. The other white meat. Let's check it out."

I follow after her, dragging my feet in the dry dirt. Won't Vovó wonder why Filipe isn't here with me? Will she think it's strange? Or did she hear about what happened earlier this week? Did Filipe tell his parents? Did Anibal?

But when we're up at the window, I can tell she hasn't heard a word about the fight because she gives me a big smile and talks excitedly with Audrey about the great food at their booth. "Oh, you must try *bifana*," she says to Audrey. "It's Drew's favorite. Two *bifana*!" she shouts back into the prep area.

Filipe's grandma turns to me. "I haven't seen Filipe at the fair yet. Is he with you?"

I shake my head. Just hearing his name makes my right hand ache. It never bruised exactly, but it is kind of sore when I think about it.

"Well." Vovó glances at Audrey just as one of the women from the kitchen slides our two plates of pork sandwiches in front of her. "It's sure nice of you to show Audrey around. Hope to see you later this summer. You better not miss our Labor Day barbecue! I want a rematch at cornhole."

Filipe and I creamed her and his vovô last summer. I don't know what to say back to her, though. What if Filipe doesn't want me to come to their Labor Day barbecue anymore? Maybe he wants to bring Theo this year. Maybe that fight was it between us. The end of everything.

I reach into my pocket for some of the cash Mom gave me.

"Oh, no, no, no," Vovó says. "Those two are on the house."

"Thank you," I say.

"See you around, Drew! Nice to meet you, Audrey."

We take our sandwiches over to an empty picnic table. Vovó's *bifana* is my favorite. Even though I don't know what's going on with Filipe lately, the first bite I take into the sandwich, it's like everything bad just melts away. There's nothing like sweet caramelized onions and salty mustard on top of the juiciest pork loin. Brown juiciness drips down my chin, but I don't stop to wipe it when I see Audrey's in the same boat as me. Funny, I never pictured her as someone who could be a messy eater.

"What do you think?" I say when I finally finish chewing.

"Beats chocolate-covered opossum any day."

Now I'm rolling my eyes at Audrey. She hands me a napkin and I wipe my face and hands.

"Okay, so I'm not hungry anymore," Audrey says. "But I *am* thirsty."

I point to a familiar cart with a green-and-yellow awning. "Want to get Del's and then go check out the farm animals?"

"Deal."

This time I don't have to tell her which flavor to

order. She knows. On our way over to the animal barns, I catch that she's really improved her slurping technique. I'd almost call her a natural. *Almost.*

"Hey, Audrey," I say, just before the brain freeze hits.

"Yeah?"

"I'm sorry about what I said last week at the library. It wasn't nice. I don't even think that about you anyway. I don't really know why I said it." It's funny how the words tumble out with Audrey, but when I'm with Filipe, they get all stopped up. "Anyway—it doesn't matter why I said it or didn't, just that I'm sorry."

Audrey goes quiet for a few seconds, though maybe she's just enjoying her Del's. Mine is a really good one, one of the best ever. Top five for sure.

"Thanks, Drew."

She doesn't have to say anything more than that. We slurp our way over toward the barn with the rabbits and chickens. We're nearly there when Audrey grabs my arm. "You weren't kidding," she says. To the right of her is the station with the huge mother cows. Their stomachs look so heavy I'm surprised they didn't give birth months ago. Hung from the rafters are flat-screen TVs in case the crowd gets too big, and everyone's craning their neck for a view.

"Of course I wasn't," I say. Did she think I just made up a cow birth joke on the fly?

A tall man in denim overalls and a Red Sox cap turns around. "Just missed a good one," he says.

Audrey makes a face like she just ate a whole lemon. "Maybe let's save the cow births for later."

Chickens and rabbits are probably the better way to ease her into the cultural experience, anyway. They're in one of the biggest barns, I guess because there are a heck of a lot more types of chickens and rabbits than there are cows. Row and rows of them, each in their own cage. There's a little card attached to each that talks about which farm it's from, how old it is, and what breed.

Once we're a few steps in, the smell gets kind of intense. Sawdust and animal poop. I'm used to it after years of coming to the fair, but I worry it's too much for Audrey.

She sucks in a gaspy breath, and I expect her to complain about the smell when she catches me off-guard. "They're so beautiful," she exclaims, marching right toward the chickens. "Drew, look!"

I hurry up and follow her over to a fluffy white one. A Silkie bantam, it says on the card. I can barely see its little black beak peeking out from under all those feathers. It's like it's part chicken, part . . . cat? Part stuffed animal?

"People in Rhode Island have chickens?" Audrey says.

"This family down the street from me has a coop in their backyard, and when they're out of town, we get to collect the eggs." I don't tell her that their chickens look more like normal chickens, not this glorious fluffy white chicken model.

"Do you think *I* could get one?"

"I don't think my mom's going to let you take a chicken home in the car tonight."

"Not *today*, Drew." She takes a picture of the little card stuck to the cage, which has contact information about the chicken's owner. "We never had much of a backyard in the other places I lived. But we do here." The chicken sticks its neck out like it's examining Audrey. I can tell part of her wants to reach in and pet it, but the other part is worried her finger might get pecked off.

She steps back from the cage. "There are so *many*. I could spend all night here."

"I told my mom we'd meet up with her and Xan at eight for the concert."

"Not literally, Drew." Audrey eyes the next chicken. It's not as pretty as the white one, but it is more talkative.

We stay in the chicken half of the barn for at least forty-five minutes as Audrey falls in love with a dozen different chickens.

Finally I see the time and remind her we've got to go meet up with my mom and Xander.

On Friday and Saturday night at the fair, a musician or band from back when Mom was young plays on the main stage. Tonight it's some band called Third Eye Blind. I've never heard of them, but Mom was very insistent on the car ride over that we needed to set down our blanket and claim a spot on time this year. Which was maybe referring to last year when Filipe and I got in a too-long line for the Ferris wheel and met up with them fifteen minutes late.

We meet Mom and Xander at eight on the dot, exactly where she said. "You guys having fun?" she asks. Xander's hugging a stuffed Pikachu that I have a feeling Mom spent too much money trying to win for him in one of those rigged carnival games. His face is painted half Spider-Man, half tiger. "Someone was indecisive this year," she says with a laugh as she pats Xander's back.

"This fair is incredible," Audrey says, answering for the both of us.

"I'm so glad you're enjoying yourself," Mom says. "We're always happy to have you tag along."

"She even found a chicken she wants to buy." I help Mom stretch out the fleece blanket in a good spot not too far back from the stage.

"Chickens, huh?" Mom smooths down the blanket, then takes a seat, stretching her legs out.

"Actually, three different ones." Audrey is careful to make sure every part of herself is on the blanket, and not the grass, as she sits down. "My favorites were the white Silkie bantam, the Barred Plymouth Rock, and the dominique."

I sit down between Audrey and Mom, making sure not to sit too close to Audrey and give Mom the wrong idea.

"If she's getting a chicken, can I get one too?" Xander asks.

"Xan, you are a chicken." Mom ruffles his hair. "And Audrey's got to check with her parents before getting a chicken. I drive a chicken-free car and I'd like to keep it that way."

"Of course," Audrey says. "I plan to do a lot more research first. You can't ask your parents for something like a chicken without doing your research."

Oh, Audrey.

When Third Eye Blind takes the stage, Mom and all the other adults start screaming, but all I can do is watch this family with a blanket set up in front of us. There's a mom and dad with their teenage son. He's off to the side, flipping through his cell phone like this fair is the absolute last place he wants to be tonight.

His dad's really getting into the music, too. Waving his hands, singing right along with the band, bopping his head. Maybe the son thinks his dad is too embarrassing, too dorky.

But if it were Phil? If Phil were my dad, I wouldn't turn away. I'd never take it for granted, how good it felt to be embarrassed by my dad. How good it felt to have a dad.

I wouldn't even care why he'd left before. So long as this time he stayed.

23

LATE SATURDAY NIGHT, I WAKE UP

to the *thrum-thrum* of Phil's motorcycle pulling into our driveway, followed by Mom's footsteps on the stairs as she goes down to let him in.

He's back. There's a tingling feeling in my arm. Maybe it's because I slept on it funny and it's just waking up, or maybe it's something more. Like my arm knows—remembers—flailing in the air with him that morning out in the backyard.

I roll over in bed to check the clock. Even though it's eleven, I want to see him. Maybe I should go down for a glass of water. Downstairs, they're talking. Not the quiet nighttime whispers Mom and Dad used to use 'cause they were afraid of waking Xander and how long it took to get him back to sleep, but normal daytime voices.

Walking down the hallway, I peek into my brother's room. His arms are splayed out, his panda bear, Mr. Diaperpants (don't ask), beneath his feet.

I sit at the top of the stairs, hugging my knees to my chest, and listen.

"It was amazing, Kay. These people, they hear Andy's story and they open their doors to me. I didn't know how deeply his story would affect them. I didn't . . . I'm so glad I did this, you know?"

It grows quiet for a moment. I can't go downstairs and interrupt this. If only I could go down there without being seen. Wear an invisibility cloak or something. Except, no, I guess I don't wish that. What do grown-ups do when they get quiet, anyway? (Kiss?) No. Ugh. No! Not that. Maybe it's one of those uncomfortable silences. It has to be.

"So, how long till you have to hit the road again?" Mom asks.

"Just can't wait to get rid of me, huh?"

Before, I would've said, *Yes. Please. Leave right now.* But now?

Stay.

"That's not it at all. Quite the opposite, actually."

Quiet again. Too quiet. There's a lump in my throat. I try to swallow it away, but it stays right there. I shift and the stairs creak below me. *Oops.*

Holding my breath, I listen closely for any movement downstairs. I could hop right up and be in my bed, fifteen seconds flat. They'd never know if it was me or Xan. I could pretend to sleep. After Dad died, I got to be an expert at that.

But nobody moves.

"I didn't realize how much I'd missed it," Mom says. "Not being the only adult in the house. It feels unbalanced, you know? It was that much more obvious once you'd left."

"How long has it been?"

"Almost three and a half years."

"Jeez, Kay."

"I know. It feels like forever ago. And then . . . some days, like it was just yesterday."

"Have you—have you seen anyone?"

"A therapist? Of course."

"No—I mean, have you dated?"

"I've been out on a few dates. Internet dates." She laughs. "It's almost comical how these guys present themselves online, and then when they actually show up in the restaurant, it's like two completely different people. Not like you."

Silence, again. Part of me wants to run down there and stop them. But the other part is frozen in place, not sure what's going to happen next. Afraid if I say the wrong thing, I'll scare Phil off and he'll bolt. And that can't happen, not if he's my real dad. I can't let that happen all over again.

"I'm serious. I know it's Facebook, but you . . . you're more honest. Not trying to pretend your life is fun and picture-perfect one hundred percent of the time."

"I didn't realize you looked."

"Of course I looked."

"No—I mean, you never liked anything or commented."

"Well, wouldn't that be creepy? I don't know, Phil. These things weren't around when we were teens. I don't know what I'm doing half the time. Or what the conventions are."

"You never cared for the conventions back then."

"No, I guess I didn't."

"We both didn't."

The quiet again. I close my eyes and try to imagine back to when it was Dad on the couch down there with Mom. She'd nag him for always bringing work home. Trying to stay up on the latest exciting developments in the world of dentistry. Couldn't he just leave work at work? To get him to put that stuff away, she'd turn on one of their favorite shows—the kinds they only watched once Xan and I were in bed. I'd fall asleep to the muffled sounds of the TV, of Mom and Dad laughing, Mom shrieking every now and then because something was too horrifying or funny or—well, who knows.

But the whole thing feels like a lie now. Dad lying to Mom. Pretending he was fine, happy. Dad lying to us.

Or worse.

Could it have really been Mom lying to me too? Letting Dad pretend he was my real dad when the whole time it was Phil? All this time? I can't even let myself think that thought seriously for too long. It's too much. Too big. Too scary.

"I should get going."

"Tonight? Are you kidding?"

"I made a reservation down the road."

"Oh, don't be serious."

"It's too much. With your kids, me being here. Maybe not for Xander, but for Drew."

Because I acted like I hated him? Or because . . . because what?

"Plus, the guest room's still made up. And Xan, he'll turn inside out just seeing you in the morning. Please?"

"Well, okay."

"It's important for Drew to spend time with you. He needs this," Mom says. "Even if it's difficult."

I hear them getting up from the sofa, and I know I have to move. By the time I'm back under the covers, my heart hammers in my rib cage.

Footsteps on the stairs. Doors open and shut. Water runs as Phil washes up in the bathroom.

One more door closing. And then the quietest quiet fills the house again.

The next morning I wake up to the birds chirping in the oak tree outside my window as the sun comes up. It's almost like my body did this on purpose. Like there's something pulling me out of bed, tugging me outside to find Phil in the backyard and ask him for the truth myself.

I peek into the hallway, but the door to his room is still closed.

All of the doors are closed except for the one leading to the bathroom.

I lie back on my bed, trying hard to stay awake, waiting for the sound of his door opening. I wait and I wait and I wait, but it never opens.

And then I fall back to sleep.

When I wake up again, I can't believe what my clock says. Nine a.m. On a Sunday? Are you kidding me?

I dart into the hall. All the bedroom doors are open now, but the bathroom door is closed because someone's taking a shower. I knock on the door. "Mom?"

"In the shower, bud. Be out in a few."

I scramble down the stairs and find my brother on the floor surrounded by Legos and Playmobil and race cars. *Curious George* plays on the TV. "Where's Phil?" I ask him.

Xander shrugs.

I peer out the window. His bike is gone. "Did he leave for good?"

Xan stares at the TV. The man in the yellow hat is angry with George. When is the man in the yellow hat ever not angry with George?

"Xan?"

Nothing.

"Xan!"

Nothing.

"XANDER."

The episode ends and he turns to me. "What?"

"Did he leave for good?"

"He went to . . ." Xan scratches his head. "I . . . forget?"

"You're hopeless!"

"I have hope." Xan stares back at me with a confused look on his face. "I do too have hope."

"Xan, it's just—it's an expression." I take the stairs two at a time and bang on the bathroom door.

"Almost done, bud. Just toweling off."

Steam pours into the hallway as Mom steps out, one towel wrapped around herself and another on her head. "Is the downstairs toilet clogged again?"

"Huh?"

"Oh, so you just wanted me to see your cute face. . . . Good morning to you too, bud." She tries to ruffle my hair, but I shirk her off. "Hon, what is it?"

"Did he leave again?"

"Phil? Oh no, did we wake you up last night?"

"It's okay—I just . . . Is he gone for good?"

Mom looks at me funny. Then she shakes her head, and something calms down inside of me. "Phil's got some stuff to do this morning, but he's planning on joining us for lunch. We'll meet up at the new Mexican place that just opened down on Maple. Sound good?"

Mexican always sounds good. "Yeah."

"Is that it? Is there something else you want to talk about?"

"Nope," I say, swallowing down all the questions before they bubble out.

Mom reaches a hand up to adjust her towel. Her left hand. I always thought it would be so strange not to see that plain silver band, stacked with that big sparkly diamond, but somehow it looks normal, seeing her finger bare. "Do you want me to make you some eggs once I'm dressed?"

"Nah. I'll get some cereal."

She pads down the hall to her bedroom, the door shutting with a click.

I head for the stairs, suddenly as hungry as I've ever been.

WE—MOM, XANDER, AND I—BEAT

Phil to the Cantina. The host seats us at a booth by the front window even though we're missing someone in our party.

Party of four, not three. Is that where this is all going? Does Mom want us to be a party of four again?

Xander plays with the hot sauces, making them dance and having them argue over which one is the hottest. Mom can't stop fiddling with the paper covering the top of her straw, finally taking it off and sipping. She checks her phone again. "Sorry, guys. He should be here any minute."

Me, I'm staring out the window. Phil wouldn't just leave town, would he? Although it does seem like the kind of thing you do on a motorcycle. Make a clean getaway.

Maybe that's what he thinks he needs to do. Maybe in his head it seemed easy to come back into town and finally tell me the truth, but maybe he chickened out. Maybe he's heading back to Colorado, never to see any of us again. I wonder what Mom would do then. Would she start with the online dating all over again?

The bell rings by the door and Phil makes his way over to us, his hand reaching up to wave at Xan. Xan waves back, a hot sauce bottle still in his hand. I can't stop a smile from spreading over my face, knowing that he didn't leave. He's here. Right here. With us.

Phil slides in next to Mom, across from my brother and me.

"Sorry for keeping you guys waiting." He takes a sip from his water. "Who's hungry for some burrrrritos?"

"Me!" Xan enthusiastically bangs the hot sauce bottles on the table. Mom snatches them away and puts them back in the little metal holder.

Phil scratches at his neck, and that's when I notice. Something's changed with him too. His beardy scruff—he's shaved it off. He looks cleaner now. Less like a guy who drives around on a motorcycle and more like . . . more like Dad, actually.

The server stops by to take our drink orders, and Phil asks for guacamole and chips and salsa for the table, but the whole time I'm not even thinking about how much I want a Dr Pepper. Instead I'm watching Phil. Phil and Mom. Mom's fingers, tapping on the table, that sparkly diamond catching the light. Wait a sec—when did she put the rings back on? After the shower? Phil fidgets with his napkin.

The server leaves us for the kitchen. Party of four again.

Phil clears his throat. "So I've been doing a lot of thinking the past couple days. That's the thing about being on the bike, right? All that time alone with your thoughts."

I take a sip from my ice water, but it goes down the wrong way, causing me to cough.

"You okay there, buddy?" Phil asks.

"Yeah," I reply in between coughs, though of course the truth is no. *Time alone with your thoughts?*

He's not going to tell me the truth *now*, is he? At a Mexican restaurant, with my brother and everything?

"Anyway, one of the things I've been thinking about is how much I've enjoyed my time in New England. Especially out by the ocean. Coastal Maine, Massachusetts, Rhode Island. It's quite a contrast to the mountains I'm used to back in Colorado. For almost a whole year now, I've been on the road. I've seen it all, so to speak. My sabbatical from teaching only lasts the year, so I've got to go back, but I've been thinking about coming out this way next summer."

For a second there, I thought he was going to say he wanted to move here. To stay.

Mom leans back in her seat. "Really?" She's got this smile on her face, bigger than I've seen in—actually, I can't remember the last time I saw her smile like that.

"Now, I don't want to put you all out again. I'm sure there are plenty of great Airbnbs. Just wanted to let you know that I'm thinking about it. And that I appreciate the hospitality . . . and the company."

The server returns with our drinks and takes our orders. The Dr Pepper hits me fast and the cold makes my teeth ache, for a second distracting me from what

Phil just said. He's still leaving—he's a grown-up with a job, after all—but . . . he might come back. *Next summer.* I can't wait a whole year to know.

Xander blurts out, "You're going to come back?"

He's always a few steps behind.

"Next summer," Phil says. "If you'll have me." He and Mom catch each other's eyes.

"Well, that would be—" Mom takes a sip of her horchata. Her eyes start to water, even though the server hasn't brought out the salsas yet. She stands up from the table. "I'll be right back, guys." She nearly walks into a server carrying dirty dishes. "Sorry! So sorry about that."

"Is Mom okay?" Xander asks me.

"She's fine," I tell him. Though the truth is, I don't know. It's almost like the second Phil mentioned coming back, she cycled through every emotion possible. From excited and maybe a little bit in love to overwhelmed and possibly sad to—well, honestly, by the end she mostly looked panicked.

I meet Phil's gaze, wondering if he's thinking what I'm thinking—that one of us should go check on Mom. But before either of us does anything, the server returns.

"And here's your guacamole and chips. Now, as for the salsas, the green one's mild, but that red one, now watch out, because that one has some kick." Our server lays it out in the center of the table, the kind of spread I could easily devour in five minutes.

All three of us just sit there and stare at it.

Xander jabs me in the ribs and whispers, "Do we have to wait for Mom?"

I shake my head. "She'll be back soon. Go on, have a chip."

Xan picks out a small one and digs it through the guacamole, nabbing a huge chunk of avocado. Sure enough, it's not even halfway to his mouth when the guac splatters onto the table.

Xan stares at me.

I stare back at Xan.

"Five-second rule?" Xan asks.

"Sure." With another chip to assist, I get that guac back on his chip. Way more than five seconds have passed, but it's not like anyone's got a timer going.

Xan munches happily. Phil still hasn't grabbed even one chip. He's staring off into the back of the restaurant, probably searching for Mom.

If I were her daughter, I probably would have gone

after her by now. But I'm way too old to wander into a women's room on purpose.

Phil finally reaches out for a chip, dipping it in the spiciest salsa. "Ooh," he says, waving in front of his mouth. "You're going to like that one, Drew."

I glance up at him, searching in those brown eyes. You can see them better than you could Dad's. No glasses in the way.

No glasses.

When do people get glasses, anyway? Is eyesight . . . Is it hereditary?

I stare out the window, focusing on the leaves, reading the sign across the street, the smallest letters. Twenty-twenty. Perfect vision, like always. Not like Dad.

But Mom doesn't have glasses, not even after reading tons of books and staring at a computer screen all day at the library. So maybe—maybe I just inherited her good eyesight.

Mom slides back into her seat like nothing ever happened. "Oh, chips and salsa!" She rubs her hands together. "Doesn't this hit the spot?"

"Sorry about that," she says to Phil, shifting in her chair. "We'd love to have you come out for a week or so next summer. There's so much you didn't see. With more time, we can make sure to show you our favorite spots, right, boys?"

"Like the zoo?" Xander says. "And a baseball game. They give you ice cream in a hat!"

"In a real hat?" Phil asks.

"No!" Xander giggles. "It's a small one."

"A plastic hat," I clarify.

"I figured," Phil says. "They serve those at Rockies games too."

"When are you going back?" I ask. "To Colorado, I mean."

Phil doesn't look right at me when he answers; he looks at Mom. "I was thinking Tuesday morning, assuming the weather's good. That all right with you?"

It only leaves one day for the yearbook to get here. It's cutting it awfully close.

"We'll be sad to see you go, but I guess it had to happen eventually, right?" I'm surprised when Mom glances at me as she says it, not Phil. Does she think he wouldn't leave if I knew he was my dad? That then he would stay? Or what?

Phil doesn't say anything back.

The server stops by to tell us our burritos should

be out soon, and tops off our tortilla chips. They're warm and oily. I snag a big, curly chip—perfect for dipping—and pop the whole thing in my mouth. The habaneros in the salsa light my tongue on fire and my eyes smart. The best kind of tears come from food.

"Good, right?" Phil offers up a closed-mouthed smile.

I let the fire shift to my esophagus. "It's great."

25

AFTER LUNCH, PHIL HEADS INTO

Warwick to pick up something he needs for his bike.
Mom, Xander, and I drive back home. I sit up front
next to Mom.

There's a craft fair on the town common, causing
a big traffic backup. We've barely moved for ten minutes and Mom keeps changing the radio station, trying to find music instead of the same old commercials.

"Do you think later today I can ride on the motorcycle?" Xan asks. "Please, Mom? Please?"

She gives up and leaves it on an oldies station.

"Maybe if Phil promises to go really slow down a cul-de-sac. But we'll need to find you a helmet first."

"Yesss! Yesss! Can Drew come too?"

Mom glances at me. "I'm sure Drew can come if he wants to." She lowers her voice. "How are you doing, bud? You've been quiet ever since we got in the car."

"I'm just full," I say. It's the truth even if it isn't the whole truth.

"Well, you didn't *have* to finish Xan's burrito. We could have had them wrap it up to take home."

"No, no. It was good. I'm just . . ."

You know how there are those Sundays during the school year where it hits you right around six o'clock how much you don't want it to be Monday tomorrow? This is the exact opposite of that feeling. I want it to be Monday so bad it actually makes my stomach hurt. The burrito—okay, one and a half burritos—they aren't bothering me so much. It's the wanting that hurts.

"Drew?"

"Yeah?"

"You know we can talk, you and I, if there's anything you want to talk about. I know this whole visit with Phil didn't go exactly as I imagined, and that it threw you for a loop at first. But I really appreciate

• 243 •

how you've handled everything since he came back. It shows a lot of maturity."

Up ahead the police officer directing traffic waves a bunch of us through.

"Is that Audrey?" Mom points to the sidewalk. A short man with gray hair and a beard and glasses and, oh yeah, that's totally Audrey.

She toots the horn twice.

"Mom!" I shout.

Audrey scrunches her nose, looking left and right, trying to figure out who's honking at her.

I turn my head so she won't see me as we pass by.

"Oh, Drew. I didn't know. I'm sorry," Mom says.

We stop at a red light, a block down from where we saw Audrey.

"Didn't know what?"

"Do you have feelings—"

"Ew. Mom. No. Stop." I slide down in my seat and turn away from her. I try to melt my body into the door of the car, but it doesn't seem to be working because somehow I'm still here and Mom's still trying to talk to me about what happened.

"I'm sorry. I just—without your dad, I didn't know when was the right time to . . ."

If Audrey really is just a friend, I'm not supposed to feel like this. Yeah, it's embarrassing for my mom to honk at her out of nowhere, but not *this* embarrassing. I'm not supposed to feel it everywhere, the way you do when you have a crush on someone. Where it just takes over, like an alien temporarily hijacking your body. I cannot explain that feeling to my mom. Not now. Maybe not ever.

"Not in the car, okay? Jeez. Xander's back there." My one and a half burritos twist together in my stomach.

When we finally pull into the driveway, I'm the first one out of the car.

"Drew," Mom calls after me.

I run to the bathroom, wishing that what I actually needed to do was poop forever. Seriously. That would be better than talking to my mom right now. I slam the door behind me and sit down on the closed toilet seat.

I can't talk to my mom about girls.

Who am I kidding?

I can't talk to my mom about any of these things. Me and Mom, we're different. She's always been so outgoing, getting along with everyone. She probably had a million boyfriends before Dad. And when it comes to the friends stuff, she and Julia never, ever fight.

Dad was more like me. More quiet and in his own head. He'd get what this is like, how I feel about Audrey, about Filipe—everything. Even him.

Except he's not here. So I guess he won't.

I hear the door open and Xander's flip-flops as they smack on the floor. He comes to a stop outside the bathroom. "I'm sorry I made you eat my burrito and go number two."

He really thinks *that's* why I'm in the bathroom. What I wouldn't give to be just six and a quarter again. "It's okay," I say.

"Me and Mom are going to the pool. Do you want to come?"

"I think I'll stay behind."

"You sure?"

"I don't think I should go in the pool like this."

"Okay."

Smack-smack-smack.

I get up from the toilet and flush. And then I stand in front of the mirror and stare back at my reflection. I know it's me, but the thing is, the longer I stare, the more foreign the person staring back at me begins to look. Almost like someone I've never seen before. That person can't be me.

I look at my ears. Really look at them. Their shape, the cartilage, the lobe, the tiny hairs on the lobe.

And my nose. My nostrils—not triangular like Xan's, but oval-shaped. The freckles on the bridge.

My eyebrows, not as thick as Filipe's but not as thin as Mom's, either.

I look at my face, the whole thing. How my ears and nose and eyes and eyebrows and cheekbones make a whole.

Who's looking back at me in the mirror?

Am I Dad's son?

Or am I Phil's?

I'm in there so long that by the time I'm finally ready to leave, I actually do have to go to the bathroom.

After, as I'm lathering up my hands with soap, I remember where there is a candid picture of Dad.

Mom didn't erase him from our life. Not all at once. But he disappeared, little by little. We all let him. The family photos in the living room that used to have the four of us got updated, the pictures in the frames replaced—all except our baby pictures.

I head up the stairs to my brother's room and pick through his bookshelf until I find it.

Alexander McCormack's Kindergarten Book.

Each kid wrote a book about themselves—well, "wrote"—and glued photographs inside. Pictures of their family, their house, their pets, favorite animals. The pages are laminated and spiral-bound.

Xander is not even a year old, sitting on Dad's lap at the Fourth of July parade in Bristol. He's drooling onto Dad's hand and Dad is smiling like he doesn't care at all. And it's a lot of drool. Like, really, he should get a towel or a napkin or something.

He doesn't look like me at all.

Or maybe . . . maybe he does?

I can't tell. In the way back of my mind, there's this stupid doubt that I can't shake off. What if the yearbook comes in time and I can't tell if Phil could really be my dad or not? What will I do then?

I stare back down at the photo of my dad. *My* dad?

I turn the page to a picture of the three of us from the last Halloween when we were all together. Xan was an Ewok, Dad was dressed as Han Solo, and then there was me with a scowl on my face, the world's grumpiest R2-D2.

Halloween was Dad's favorite holiday. He loved everything about it—telling scary stories, the candy (even candy corn, which, ick), and especially making costumes. In the evenings, we'd hang out in the shed, just Dad and me. Sketches of his costume ideas and inspirations were pinned up on the walls. He'd take all my measurements and try out the different pieces to make sure they wouldn't rub my neck or fall apart once I started walking around. He let me help too, always finding some part of the costume that wouldn't be too hard for a little kid to help paint or decorate. The only way to really do Halloween, he said, was to make your costume yourself. And so we did, every year. I'd hang out in there with Dad, with some warm cider or hot cocoa, and the hours would just disappear.

Except that year. That last Halloween, he kept putting it off. He'd say, we'll work on the costume *next* weekend. And then next weekend would come and he'd be too tired from work, but he'd promise we'd get to it the following weekend. But then we had only one weekend left before Halloween. Dad promised. That weekend we'd get it done, even if it took all day Saturday and Sunday. I was ready, too. Excited. I had visions of it in my head—how I'd look so much like the real R2-D2 you'd have to do a double-take.

But when I got up on Saturday morning, his car

wasn't in the driveway and Mom told me he had an emergency surgery. But—*but!*—she said, she'd found the perfect R2-D2 costume online and they were rush-shipping it so it'd be here just in time for Halloween.

As if that made any of it okay.

Mom didn't get it—not at all. That it wasn't about the costume. It was about that time with Dad, that time alone, just the two of us making something amazing.

That was our last Halloween together. And he ruined it.

I peer closely at Han Solo Dad's face. Did he know then what he was going to do just a few months later?

I hate that I can't tell. That I'll never know. That there was so much going on behind that face that looked so happy most of the time.

I place the book back on the shelf, exactly where I found it.

Xander's bed is unmade. It would have driven Dad crazy. He needed stuff to be in order, my dad. But Xander never even got to know that about him.

All he has is that picture in his book. And stories I don't even tell him. Stories I keep locked up inside.

Someday he won't even have a single memory of Dad. You don't remember being that little.

Maybe that's better, though. Not remembering. Because there are good memories and there are bad, and you don't get to choose which ones stick in your brain forever.

I open the door to the guest room. There's this new smell, the smell of Phil, I guess: pine needles and fresh grass. Maybe he brings the outdoors inside after all that time on his bike. The sheets are tucked in, the comforter smoothed over. Is Phil that tidy? Or did Mom do it for him, like she does for me when Grandma comes to town?

I check the pillow quick, hoping for a stray hair just in case. But there's not even a single brown curly hair on the pillowcase. Aside from the smell, there's no sign that Phil stayed here last night except for a navy-blue backpack on the chair in the corner.

I should not look in it. It's his. I have no right.

I glance back at the door. In the months after Dad died, I used to have this feeling that he was watching me. Not like a ghost, exactly. More like how some people think of God. I haven't had it in a while, though, but it's back.

Just a little peek. Nothing more.

I unzip the front pouch. Pens and pencils. A sunglasses case. A pocket-size blue spiral notebook. I flip through it. Man, Phil's handwriting is terrible. How can anyone read something like that? Anyway, there are just a few little notes—names and phone numbers—and the rest is blank.

I make sure everything is exactly as I found it and zip it back up.

Next, the main compartment. A Deep Springs College sweatshirt. And two books. An extremely worn motorcycle manual and a thick George R. R. Martin paperback with a superlong CVS receipt folded up about halfway through.

Thrumm-thrumm-thrumm.

Yikes!

I scramble to put everything back in and zip it up. I slam the door to his room and nearly trip running down the stairs.

It's only when I'm at the front window that I realize it isn't Phil at all. Just my next-door neighbor, Mr. Quintana, firing up his lawn mower. Black smoke gushes out of the thing, and it sputters down.

My heart sputters down too.

What was I even hoping to find in his backpack anyway? A letter to me confessing the truth? Pffft. No way.

Unless I can snag something with his DNA (and come up with whatever money it takes to get one of the kits), the yearbook is our best lead. Maybe there's even a picture in there of him and Mom. Something that proves she's been lying about at least one thing, so maybe she's lying about more.

Audrey and I *will* get to the bottom of this. I just hope we can in time.

MONDAY MORNING THE TEEN LIBRARIAN

calls in sick, so Mrs. Eisenberg heads upstairs to cover for her. They're short-staffed today; half the librarians, including my mom, went to Newport for an all-day conference.

A magician's coming this afternoon for a family program, so there's no story hour this morning and the children's room is oddly quiet. I'm mostly ready for Wednesday's story hour—*Battle Bunny*—except I still need to make the name tags.

Since the book is all about messing with Little

Golden Books, I'm taking different well-known characters, like the Poky Little Puppy, and photocopying them to make name tags. It's time-consuming, but Mrs. Eisenberg said that was okay. Sometimes I think she worries she's going to run out of stuff for me to do, so she doesn't mind if my projects get a little, as she says, *involved*.

Audrey is upstairs helping the reference librarians.

Sometimes when it's so quiet down here, I wish we could play music. Why is it that there's always music playing softly at the grocery store or a doctor's office, but never the library?

Feet thump in the stairwell, and then Audrey bursts through the door, clutching her stomach.

"Are you . . . sick?" I grab the papers from the copy machine and take them over to a table.

"Sick? No, Drew. It's here." She reaches under her shirt, pulling out a thin, dark green book.

The yearbook.

Audrey rushes over to the table and pulls out a chair. I sit down next to her.

"It came," I say.

Deering High School Yearbook, 1995. I trace my fingers over the gold indented letters on the cover.

"What are you waiting for? Aren't you going to open it?"

"Give me a sec, okay?"

Last night at supper, Xander got weirdly sniffly about Phil leaving again. But me, I just couldn't take my eyes off him. I think Mom noticed too. Like she was watching me watch him. Does she wonder if I've figured it out? Does she think that's why I'm being a lot nicer to Phil this time?

If we open the yearbook, and I find my proof and tell them I know, will he change his mind and stay?

"Drew?"

"Yeah?"

Audrey reaches out for my free hand and gives it a squeeze. "It's going to be okay."

But maybe it's not, I think, squeezing back, my hand cold and clammy. Audrey doesn't know the truth. She never knew my dad. She still thinks he's alive.

There are no takebacks here. Dad will never be able to explain himself—or this—or anything. That's all history.

I glance at the clock. We don't have forever for this. In half an hour, another librarian will take over in the teen room and Mrs. Eisenberg will return to the children's room and we'll have to be done.

It's going to be okay.

Like I have another choice?

I let go of Audrey's hand and crack open the yearbook. She pulls her chair closer to me, so close I can hear her breathing through her nose. Short, fast breaths. Unfamiliar faces stare back at us from black-and-white pictures. I don't know where to start.

Okay, not with the teacher section.

"Is there an index?" Audrey asks.

Right. The index. I flip to the back, and sure enough, there is. I scan through the *P*s until I find it. *Pittman, Philip.*

"Whoa—he must've done a lot of stuff," Audrey says.

"Huh?"

"He's on twelve different pages. That's a lot."

She's right. Most of the other names only have a few pages listed, not a dozen.

I grab a pencil and scribble down the page numbers on the back of a name tag.

"He must have been popular," Audrey says as I flip to the first page listed, thirty-seven.

I shrug.

Page thirty-seven is in the special section for

graduating seniors. Some of the pictures look like they were taken by professional photographers; others, not so much.

"Hey, that's your last name." Audrey points to the top of page thirty-six. "Funny. I wonder if there are any Nussbaums."

I nearly drop the book. Staring back at me is my dad. James Leonard McCormack. What's he doing in here?

"Oh my gosh. Look at Phil's hair! So much of it." Audrey's laughing, but my eyes are still stuck on that picture of my dad. He didn't wear glasses back then, and his brown hair was parted in the middle. (It was not a good look.) But he's smiling and he looks nerdy, though not so nerdy that he couldn't maybe get a girl-friend. And he looks so young. Like Anibal's age, which makes sense. That's how old Anibal is now—eighteen. But how is he in *this* yearbook?

"Hey."

"Yeah?" I say, blinking. This has got to be a dream, not real life. Mom and Dad didn't know each other in high school. They met after college—in Boston. Even though they both grew up in Colorado, it was Boston that brought them together. Right? Or did I get it all mixed up? It's been years since I heard their how-we-met story.

"Don't you think Phil's hair is nuts?"

I glance at the other side, page thirty-seven, the one I'm supposed to be looking at. She's right. Phil's hair is enormous. Those brown curls pretty much fill up his whole picture.

"Yeah," I say quietly. "That's a lot of hair."

"Can we see if there are any Nussbaums? I'll be quick."

"Sure." I hand her the yearbook. She's fast, shaking her head already after checking the index. "What's the next page?" She grabs the scrap paper.

"Forty-eight."

That brings us to the class will. Maybe some people think it's funny, the idea of leaving something behind for your friends, but there's nothing funny about wills and why you leave them.

Each senior gets a fair amount of space, so my dad's isn't on this two-page spread. Just Phil's.

Always remember: Phish, DMB, Boulder adventures, Sturgis!? No, Caveman tan, KP.

Thanks to: Mom, Dad, Andy. Love you forever.

Everyone else made a collage. Teeny-tiny pictures

of their friends and family. Not Phil, though. There's just the one picture. Him, I think, dangling by his arms from a huge tree branch, with someone who looks a few years younger than him dangling too. They're just kids in the picture. Maybe even my age.

It's so small I can barely make out their faces. Can't see if either of them really looks like me.

"Caveman tan?"

I want to flip back a page or two to find Dad's, but how can I say that to Audrey? There's so much she doesn't know about my dad. And I can't stop and tell her the truth—not now.

"Page sixty-two. Coming right up." Audrey flips fast, and then we're there. A two-page spread for the fall play, *A Midsummer Night's Dream*. There's a cast picture on the right, but that's page sixty-three.

Two guys not in costume, just T-shirts, their arms slung over each other's shoulders. One has a base-ball hat on backward. The other, a pile of curly hair. Beneath the photo: *Jimmy and Phil cutting loose before rehearsal.*

There's no way—that's my dad, staring back at me. My dad . . . and Phil.

They knew each other?

I flip back to the index, checking Dad's name this time. Looking for the overlap between him and Phil. All the pages they're on together. Seventy-eight. Model United Nations. There they are again, in the back row. Right next to each other.

Page 106, the school talent show. The two of them are onstage with something on the top of their heads that makes them look like coneheads. *Future SNL stars*, the caption reads.

Sixty-five. A picture of just the two of them in running tank tops, with orange-slice smiles. Below, a quote from Phil: *We may not be the fastest, but we have the most fun.*

They didn't just know each other. They were *friends*. Maybe best friends.

I shut the book.

"Drew?"

I push back my chair. I feel—sick? Like the world under my feet is unsteady. I used to feel this way all the time three summers ago when Mom left me at rec camp. Like the earth had started spinning faster and I was the only one who could feel it.

I dash to the bathroom.

It's all coming back to me. Three years erased in a

second. I get to the toilet just in time for my stomach to empty into it. The yearbook clatters against the tile floor.

Phil and my dad—they were friends? No. No, no, *no*.

"Drew?" Audrey's outside the bathroom door. "Are you okay?"

I bite down on the inside of my cheek so hard that I puncture it. At the sink, I spit out saliva and blood.

"If you don't say anything, I'm going upstairs to get Mrs. Eisenberg. I'm serious."

"Don't," I yell back, splashing water on my face.

This wasn't supposed to happen. There were two scenarios, two, that I'd prepared myself for. For Phil's face to look like mine, enough that I could ask him and Mom. Or for Phil to look nothing like me.

I didn't know what that would feel like, honestly. Would I be disappointed? It's sort of like how you don't know your true feelings until you do a coin toss. Except this coin has three sides somehow. *Mom's old friend.* That was how she introduced Phil. But he and Dad, they were friends. No, not just friends. *Best* friends. How could Mom have left that out?

"I know it's the men's room, but I'm coming in if you don't come out! One, two—"

I push open the door.

"Drew." Audrey's wringing her hands again. It's like how she was that day with Benny, except worse. "What's wrong? Are you . . . are you sick? Wait—is he actually your dad? Phil?"

That's what she thinks?

Mrs. Eisenberg comes out the elevator door before I've answered Audrey. "Hey, Mrs. Eisenberg?"

"Yes, Drew."

"I think I'm coming down with something. Could you give me a ride home?"

"You're not feeling well?"

I shake my head.

"He threw up," Audrey adds.

Mrs. Eisenberg makes a bit of a face. "Oh, dear. Let's see about getting you home. I'll call upstairs and check if anyone's heading that way for lunch. Just a sec."

The yearbook is still lying on the bathroom floor. I run back in for it, then snag a few magazines off the spinning rack to wrap around it. I feel kind of guilty for doing it—I know I should check them out upstairs—but I'll bring them right back tomorrow.

"Looks like Pauline's heading out any second now. She can give you a ride. Do you want me to call your mom?"

"No, I'll text her." I pull out my phone and act like I'm texting her, though I never press send.

Audrey scribbles something down on a piece of paper, folds it, and places it in my hand. I stick it in my pocket without looking and head upstairs to meet Pauline.

On the short ride to my house, I pull out Audrey's note.

Call me later, okay? She's written down her phone number too.

Go figure. This would be the first time I get a girl's number.

PAULINE PULLS INTO MY DRIVEWAY.

"You sure you don't want a Gatorade or some ginger ale? I'm more than happy to swing by CVS."

"No. Thanks, though." I reach for the door handle. "I think we've got some in the fridge."

"Well, I hope you feel better, Drew. You change your mind, you just give us a holler, okay?"

"Okay."

Mom keeps a key hidden under a fake rock tucked behind some plants. I find it and wave back at Pauline.

She backs out of the driveway as I'm putting the key in the lock.

It's cool and dark inside my house, like a church. Not that I've been in years. Church was a Dad thing.

Dad.

It's got to be out there somewhere in the shed. His copy of the yearbook. Probably been there all along. I crack open the sliding glass door and slip out. The grass is crunchy, like it needs a good watering.

I fling open the door to the shed. Light streams in through the skylight overhead, catching all the tiny particles of dust stirred up from me opening the door. I slam the door behind me.

It was never Phil. It was always you. Always, always, always you.

"What else are you hiding, huh?" I shout. "You. Mom. Phil. You're all liars."

I reach for the first box I see. I drop it on my foot and kick it like I'm punting a football, kick it as hard as I can, sending it crashing it into a wall of boxes.

But it's not heavy enough to knock them over. The wall shakes, but it remains standing.

I rip another off the top and I chuck it—chuck it against the wall with whatever force is left in my body.

My arms feel weak. From puking? Or because I don't have a dad tossing footballs with me on the weekend, the way Filipe has Mr. Nunes? No one's here to teach *me* how to be a man.

I grab another box and hurl it. And then another. Glass shatters inside. Metal clangs against metal. Papers scatter, cascading all over the floor. An endless sea of paper.

All his stuff. All of it.

It's so much.

And it's nothing, too.

It's *nothing* but *stuff.*

"I hate you, you know that?"

I close my eyes and wait, like I'm leaving space for him to answer. The biggest space. The space he'll never fill.

"Maybe Xander doesn't yet. But someday he will too. Someday he'll wish someone else could be his father. Anyone but you."

My throat is raw and my stomach is growling and I'm about to drop-kick another box when I think I hear a knock on the shed door.

It's the middle of the day. Who could even be here? Mom's still in Newport.

It better not be Filipe. After how things have been with us lately, he's the last person on earth I want to see right now. If he thought me pushing and punching him was crazy, he sure shouldn't see this.

For a moment I stand perfectly still, not making a sound. If I'm totally quiet, maybe whoever it is will go away.

But then the door handle turns. And when I look behind me, it's Audrey standing in the doorway, a plastic Rite Aid bag dangling from her wrist. "He's really your dad? Phil, I mean." Her eyes meet mine. "Wait—isn't he?"

I shake my head no, my eyes darting around the shed, seeing for the first time everything as Audrey must see it. Papers everywhere. Boxes upturned. Tiny shards of clear broken glass. A big, broken, heaping mess.

Audrey chews on her lip. "But isn't that what you wanted?"

"No," I say at first. "Yes."

How can they both be wrong? How can they both be right?

"It's just . . ." I walk closer, stepping over one of the smashed boxes, something crunching beneath my sneaker. "If my real dad was Phil . . . it would mean he'd left me for twelve years. Just ditched me, let me be raised by someone else only to come back now. But—" I swipe my hand under my nose. All the things I've wanted to say aloud for so long, to somebody, anybody, rise into my chest. Fill it up where for so long it's been deflated. "At least you can fix that. There's still time."

Audrey takes a step closer to me, bridging the gap between us. She reaches out her hand, so unsure of what she's supposed to do next. But I don't take it yet. I'm not close enough. Not ready.

I shove my hands in my pockets. "He abandoned me, my dad. My real dad. He left me forever three years ago. And he's never coming back."

I wait for the confused look to spread across her face before turning into anger. Wait for that moment when she realizes who I really am. A liar, just like my dad. Wait for that moment when she backs away and leaves, that moment when she realizes she's in way, way over her head with me. I mean, look at this place.

But the moment doesn't come. Instead she says, "I know."

"No." A sob catches in my throat. "No, you don't."

But Audrey nods. "I do, Drew. I know the truth." I try to look in her eyes, but her glasses keep fogging up. "About his suicide."

No one ever says it that way—so bluntly. As if saying "he passed away" instead changes things. Except it never does. It just makes it easier for them, so *they* don't have to think about it. So *they* can pretend it away.

But Audrey isn't pretending like everyone else. And she's still here, standing right in front of me, not even bothered that I lied to her about everything, that I dragged her on this wild-goose chase only to end up in the giant mess of my dad's shed, the truth exactly what it was at the beginning.

I don't know why she does it then, except that it's sort of like Audrey to do the unexpected thing. She hands me the plastic bag. "I got Gatorade and ginger ale. I wasn't sure what you'd want."

I take out the Gatorade, the lemon-lime kind that looks like it's radioactive, and crack open the top. Over in the corner of the shed, beneath the window, are two boxes I haven't destroyed yet. They look sturdy enough to sit on.

Once we're sitting down, I gulp some Gatorade and clear my throat. "Did Mrs. Eisenberg tell you?"

"You know how you said he's a dentist?"

I nod.

"My mom needed to schedule a teeth cleaning for my dad, so I told her how your dad was a dentist and that she should look him up. She acted kind of funny about it. I forget what she said, but it left me with a weird feeling, so I . . ." She bites her lip. "I shouldn't have gone behind your back. I should have asked you. I didn't think we were going to end up friends. I just—"

Gone behind my back? "What do you mean?"

"I googled. That's how I found his obituary. It didn't include a cause of death—it was vague—so I kept looking." Audrey stares down at her feet.

"Looking . . . where?" It weirds me out a little, thinking of her digging around. Truth is, I don't know what exactly is out there. I was nine. I wasn't looking then.

"Everywhere. All the places. I—" She swipes a piece of hair out of her face. "I was supposed to stop and I didn't, okay? I was doing it all over again. I know. I *know*. I'm such a weirdo. I mean—" Audrey huffs. "Of course I was already a weirdo anyway." She closes her eyes, and for a second I notice how long her eyelashes are. Are they really that long or do her glasses make them even longer?

"Audrey, stop."

She rubs a finger under her eyes and adjusts her glasses. "What?" Her voice comes out small, un-Audrey like.

"How hard did you . . ." I try to imagine it: Audrey up late at night on her computer at home, searching and searching for stuff about my dad. The more I think about it, the less I'm weirded out. That kind of searching takes effort. Time. She did all of that . . . for me. "How'd you figure it out in the end?"

"I found this post your mom wrote on a message board a couple months after."

Mom wrote on a message board? "But how did you know what to look for?"

"You really want to know? Really?" She stares back at me, her face turning from pinkish red to a more normal pale.

I take a sip of Gatorade. "Kind of."

"I checked your mom's Facebook. But that was set to private because she's smart and everything, so then I found her Yelp page, which had her username, and then I searched that username and the word 'husband' and that's how I found the message board where she wrote about his suicide."

Whoa. That is a lot. I can't help being impressed with Audrey. She could be a private detective someday. But still, it's weird to think of her reading stuff my mom wrote, especially so soon after. She probably wrote it online because she didn't want anyone who really knew her to know what she was thinking. And maybe she still doesn't. "What did she say?"

Audrey stares out at an upturned box that used to be full of files from Dad's work. "That's the thing," she says. "When you go looking, you don't know what you're going to find. I shouldn't have seen what your mom wrote. It wasn't for me. She was sad and angry and she just wanted to find someone who would listen. I mean, of course you can find it and read it if you want to. Freedom of information and all that jazz. But think about it first. Do you *really* want to know?"

She's right. I can't find out that way. It's one thing for Audrey to see that, but another for me. If I really want to know, I need to ask Mom face-to-face.

"Audrey?"

"Yeah."

"You said you did this *before*?"

Audrey nods, and when she says, "Yeah," it's in that small voice again.

"What happened?"

"At my last school, I was the new kid again, so I thought it'd help if I knew a lot about everyone at the school. That I'd fit in. No one would need to explain things to me. But . . . it turns out that actually the people you think are your friends will stop being your friends when they discover that you Google-stalked them and already know everything about them."

I wince.

"Yeah." Audrey chews on her lip. "It's never been easy for me, making friends. Not like it was with you. At the end of August, I'll have to start all over again at a new school and . . ." Her voice keeps getting higher, like she's about to start crying. "I just don't know why it'll be any different. I mean, I haven't changed. They won't like me, I know it."

"That's not true."

"Which part?"

"All of it. Look, when we first met, it wasn't like we became instant BFFs. Things take time. But you have changed. Are you kidding me? Audrey, you held a baby. That's *huge*. And the kids at the library are totally warming up to you."

She stops chewing her lip. "Really?"

"When you were upstairs this morning, Chloe Irving came in with her mom and she said she didn't want to get her prize until you were back because you were really good at helping her choose the best one."

Audrey glances up at the ceiling. "Wait, is she the one with the adorable cat shoes?"

I nod. "See!" I finish off the Gatorade in a few gulps.

The plastic bag crinkles as Audrey takes out the can of ginger ale. "You mind if I have this?"

I let out a little laugh. "You bought it."

"Actually, my mom did."

Suddenly it occurs to me that I don't even know how Audrey got here. "Is she waiting in her car out there?"

Audrey shakes her head. "She dropped me off. I just have to call her when I'm ready to get picked up."

I'm still having a hard time believing she came out here, came after me, when that whole time I was keeping the full truth from her.

Audrey cracks the can open and ginger ale fizzes out. She brings it up to her mouth quickly, but not before a bunch spills out, trickling down her chin and wetting her shirt. She laughs at herself. "Oops."

It's so quiet I can hear the tiny bubbles tinkle against the metal of the can. It's crazy to think the whole world is just on the other side of this door. My house, Mr. Quintana's next door, Filipe's—it feels so much farther away. As if this is some kind of secret hideaway. Was that how it felt for Dad? Was that why he'd hang out in here?

"My dad," Audrey says, clearing the air, "he had this friend back in Pasadena, Bill, another scientist. Bill died from a suicide too. He lived by himself, so he used to come over to our house a lot for dinner. He and my dad would sit around the dining room table for hours talking about their experiments. Bill's the one who got me listening to Puccini. He was a total geek for opera. For a while after it happened, my dad was so sad. Almost like he felt guilty. He wished he'd been able to get Bill help, that he'd known how Bill was really feeling."

"That sucks," I say. "For your dad . . . and for Bill."

Audrey plays with the tab on her ginger ale can. "It sucks for you, too." The tab breaks off, dropping in the can unexpectedly with a *plunk*. Audrey turns to me, and for a few seconds we're just staring at each other. I can't imagine what she sees when she looks at me. My eyes are probably still red from crying—*bawling*—in front of her just a few minutes ago. I swipe again at my nose, sure somehow it's boogery from earlier.

When Filipe and I would watch a movie with a moment like this—where someone's upset and then the other one gets them to calm down and then there's this quiet pause—we'd chant, "Kiss! Kiss! Kiss!" Most of the time we were joking. "Come on!" Filipe would yell. "Make out already." One time Anibal walked into the living room during one of those scenes and cracked up at us. "Guess this is as close as you two will get for a while."

Filipe chucked a cookie at Anibal's face, barely missing. He wasn't wrong.

Now, I know Audrey's not going to kiss me. And I'm not brave enough to kiss Audrey anytime soon. But is she thinking about it the way I am? Is that why her cheeks are suddenly so red?

The door to the shed flings open. "Drew!"

My mom stands in the doorway, her hand flying to her mouth when she sees what a disaster this place has become.

She marches toward me, not bothering where she steps, her feet crunching all kinds of things.

She ignores Audrey and wraps her arms around me something fierce, a hug so tight I can barely breathe. "Mom," I struggle to say, my words muffled by her sweater.

When she finally pulls away, I notice how messy her ponytail is, like she redid it fifty times on the way home from Newport. What time is it, anyway? She's not supposed to be back until five o'clock.

"I'm just glad you're okay." Her lip quivers. She reaches up to fix her hair, like suddenly she's remembered it's a mess. "Pauline texted to let me know she'd dropped you off, something about you getting sick. But then when I texted you, you didn't reply. I called the house phone. I called over to Filipe's in case you'd gone over there, but no one answered. Drew, I didn't know what to think."

Audrey shifts on the box like she's trying to figure out her next move and Mom suddenly notices her. "Hi, Audrey," Mom says with a tiny wave.

"I brought Drew something to help settle his stomach."

"Wasn't that thoughtful of you." Mom begins to take it all in, the mess I've made of her "she shed," although I guess it really isn't a she shed yet.

Audrey stands up. "I . . . I should get going."

"Do you need a ride?" Mom asks.

"My mom can get here in a few minutes. She's close by."

"You sure?"

"I'm sure." Still holding the ginger ale can in her hand, Audrey steps carefully over the boxes, broken picture frames, papers, and loose photos until she's at the door. Mom left it ajar when she came in, the sunlight streaming in on a slant.

For a second, the light catches Audrey's hair and it looks like it's glowing. Someday, maybe not too long from now, she'll definitely be the girl who gets kissed in the movie.

"See you tomorrow?" she asks me, her hand on the door.

"Yeah. Tomorrow."

Once Audrey's gone, Mom turns to me. "Drew," she says. "What's going on?"

28

I CHEW ON THE INSIDE OF MY CHEEK

as I try to figure out where to start, the pain and confusion from earlier suddenly boomeranging back. "Why didn't you tell me the truth? Phil was Dad's best friend . . . right?"

Mom slowly nods. "How did you . . . ?"

"The yearbook."

"Was that why you were out here a couple weeks ago?"

"No," I say. "Audrey and I got it from the library. Interlibrary loan."

"Through Loretta?"

"Does it matter? Come on, Mom. Tell me. Tell me the truth. How did you and Dad and Phil all know each other?"

"I thought you knew your dad and I met in high school, Drew. That wasn't meant to be a secret. Honestly, I worried telling you too much about Phil right off the bat would give you the wrong impression."

Had I really misremembered it? Told myself a new story about them from the fuzzy details I did remember?

"Anyway, would it help to go over all of this again, from the beginning? Set the record straight?"

As I nod, Mom takes a seat on the box where Audrey had been sitting. "When I was a kid, we moved a lot. You remember that, right?"

"Yeah." The truth is, a lot of Mom's life is still sort of a mystery to me. Maybe I was too busy living my own life to wonder about it much before. I picked up bits and pieces when we all got together as a family, but if you asked me to write down my mom's life story before I was born, I'm not sure I could come up with more than a few paragraphs.

"It wasn't until high school that we settled in one place for a long stretch of time. Suddenly I was in the suburbs of Denver, the new girl in tenth grade, and I met someone. Phil."

"So he *was* your boyfriend. Why didn't you just say that?"

"That was almost thirty years ago, Drew. Never in a million years would I have thought . . ." A tiny smile creeps across Mom's face before she clears her throat. "Anyway! Phil had lived his whole life in the same town. I envied him. He'd established real roots there. Everyone in town knew him and his family.

"Phil and your dad had been best friends since they were little. Sandbox buds, like you and Filipe. Through Phil, I got to know your father, and . . . well . . . we were young, and when you're young, it's so easy to fall in love. There's no real world to contend with, not yet."

"Did you cheat on Phil with Dad?"

"Whoa! Hey now." Mom laughs.

"Well?"

"No, not exactly. But I did have feelings for your dad before I broke things off with Phil. It was complicated, Drew. They were best friends. Needless to say, Phil didn't take it well. And he and your dad, they were never close after that."

"Was Phil still in love with you?"

"He started dating Stacy Adams pretty quickly after, so . . ." Mom shrugs. "The thing is, Phil and your dad had all those years of closeness. Shared memories of times I don't know about. When we graduated and went our separate ways, I never stayed in touch with Phil. And neither did your dad. We came out to Boston for grad school and built our life here on the East Coast.

"Not long after your dad died, I signed up for Facebook. It helped, catching up with old friends. Turns out Phil had heard about Dad, but he couldn't come back for the funeral because he was teaching overseas in South Korea. We stayed in touch, loosely, in the way that you sort of know way too much about everyone if you check Facebook, and then when he mentioned he was coming out this way in the summer, I started to think that, while it would be nice for me to see him and catch up a bit, it could also be good for you to get to know him."

"Me?"

"A lot of time has passed since your dad died. Three-plus years is huge when you're still a kid, and it's natural that you're having more questions. I'm worried that you don't really remember your dad, that the way he died has colored everything you remember of him. And I thought Phil might be able to help you get to know what your dad was like when he was your age. You don't have any aunts and uncles on that side, and with Grammy in a nursing home . . .

"But then." Mom laughs. "Your reaction to Phil, when he came! Oh gosh, Drew, if you could have murdered him with your eyes . . ."

"I wasn't *that* bad."

"Drew." Mom eyeballs me.

"Okay, okay. Sorry."

She squeezes my knee. "I get it. Maybe it could have worked if he hadn't gotten here ahead of schedule, if I'd been able to do a better job preparing you. Never mind that . . ."

"What?"

"Well, I didn't bet on *liking* him. People change a lot over the years. They evolve. Phil and your dad, they took such different paths in life."

"You like Phil's path more? The motorcycle thing?"

"Actually, the motorcycle terrifies me, to be quite honest. Don't think you're getting on that thing anytime soon."

"Good luck breaking that to Xander."

There's this tingly feeling in my arms and legs, the kind that make me want to shake it out. I think I get where it comes from now. Keeping secrets.

"Can I tell you something crazy?" I ask. "You have to promise you won't tell anyone else, though. No one at the library. And not Phil, okay?"

"What is it?"

"You promise?"

Mom nods solemnly.

"I thought maybe Phil came for another reason."

"As in . . . ? I'm sorry, hon, I don't follow."

"I thought maybe—remember, you promised—maybe Phil was my real dad."

Mom is quiet for a moment when I say it, and I can feel her eyes on me even if I can't look up at her face just yet.

"I guess . . ." I stare at a knot in the wooden floor, remembering all the time I spent with Dad in here. How I'd sit up on the workbench, swinging my legs back and forth in the way that always drives Mom crazy but never bothered Dad. The way he would throw his head back and laugh, sometimes until he was crying, when I said something funny. And how we could just be quiet together, each doing our own thing, totally okay in the silence.

We were supposed to have so much more time together. It's not fair that we don't. I hate that he took that from me.

"Maybe," I say, "I kind of wanted it to be true. Because then that meant my real dad didn't kill himself."

Mom pulls me close, folding me into her arms. "Oh, I know, Drew. I know."

She holds me for a while until finally I pull away. "Do you still . . . get mad at him?"

"Not as much as I used to. Not every day anymore. There are moments sometimes—moments he should be here for. Like when you got that 'most improved in math' award at the end of the school year. Or that time two winters ago when all three of us had that stomach bug. It's never just one emotion at a time. Sometimes anger mixes with sadness. And sometimes I miss him—just *miss* him." Mom runs a finger under her bottom lashes. "Three years is a long time. But then some days it's not. And everything feels raw, you know?"

"Yeah," I say, relieved at how good it feels to agree with her. To say it aloud. "I know."

Mom reaches out and brushes the hair that hangs over my forehead. "I'm always trying to get you to tell me how you're feeling, but most of the time you never respond, bud."

"I know. I'm sorry."

"I want to be that person you come to when something's troubling you. I know for a while there it probably felt like you had to be second in command, my copilot. But I'm the mom, Drew. And you can come to me with anything. Can we try harder at that? Please?" Mom must be waiting for me to look her in the eye, because when I finally do, the corners of her mouth turn up, and she's almost smiling.

"Okay," I say. "But can you not ask me the second I'm back from school or the library? Just give me a few minutes?"

Now she's full-on smiling. "I think I can do that." She stares off into the mess for a second, like she's probably calculating how long it'll take to clean it up. "Do you remember Pop-Pop?" she asks. That's the nickname I had for my grandfather, for Dad's dad.

"Yeah," I say. He died not long after Dad. Pancreatic cancer. "I mean, kinda." We didn't make it out much to see him. And he didn't like to travel.

Mom said he was *very particular about things*.

"Growing up, your dad wasn't encouraged to be open about his feelings. Pop-Pop used to say, 'Real men don't talk about the mushy-gushy stuff. That's for the ladies.'" Mom cringes. "Sometimes I wonder if everything might've been different if your dad hadn't grown up around that kind of thinking. It's important for everyone to talk about their feelings. Boys included." I nod, though all I'm thinking is how it's not always that easy. Filipe and I used to be able to talk about all kinds of stuff, but our feelings? Really only when it was about one of our crushes, and even then, sometimes it felt kind of awkward. Like I couldn't actually tell him the real truth. Like I was performing, a little.

"One of the things I appreciate about Phil is how he's a lot more in touch with that side of himself."

"Maybe too much." I let out a little laugh.

"Maybe for some people," Mom says. "But honestly, I'll take it. Better than the opposite. The past few years, for better or for worse, between Mrs. Eisenberg and me, you've spent a lot more time around women. I was kind of hoping some of that might have rubbed off on you."

"I think it just means I get to hear about her hot flashes."

Mom laughs. "Really?"

"There was this one day last summer where she must have taken her cardigan on and off like a hundred times. I think she just wanted me to know she wasn't going crazy."

"Well, we're all a little bit of that." Mom crosses her legs.

Are we, though? Is that a part of Dad that's inside of me for sure? "Was that why he did it?" I ask. "Because he was crazy—I mean, depressed?"

"I don't think we'll ever have a real answer to—"

"No." I'm struggling to get it out there, the thing I've been so hung up on. "I mean, I get that we'll never know exactly why he did it. But, like, Dad seemed *fine*. He seemed okay. Happy. Normal. So was he just faking it? All the time?"

Mom turns to me. "I'm not sure I understand . . ."

"Was he just a liar? Or, like, a really good actor? Because I really thought he was happy. With us, I mean. But he wasn't. Right?"

"Oh, Drew. No." Mom's mouth hangs open. "No,

no, no. Is that what you've been thinking all this time?"

I sniff. "Kind of. Yeah?"

"Your dad wasn't the kind of person to struggle openly. I think that had a lot to do with how he was raised. So you're right in that sense, Drew. You didn't see that side of your dad, but I did. For a lot of years there, most of your childhood, your dad was doing a really, really good job of managing his depression. Up until the fall. But hiding a part of yourself, that's different from lying. Your dad and I—we were trying to protect you. It was out of love that we kept that from you. It doesn't mean his happiness was an act, or that the joy he found in you and Xander was pretend. Drew, none of that was pretend. None of that was a lie.

"James was doing the best he could with what he had. But I hate that it wasn't enough. And I hate that he didn't ask for help this time. And I hate that he made the one mistake you can't right. I hate that so, so, so much.

"But your dad was more than how he died. You need to know that."

I swipe under my nose again. "Okay." There's this question I've wanted to ask forever, but it never felt like the right time to ask it. But Mom wants me to not keep my feelings to myself, and maybe that means my questions too. "Have you forgiven him?"

"It took me a while to get there, but yes, Drew. I have."

As I watch Mom's face, I know one thing for sure. She's not lying. She's telling me the truth. And if she can forgive him, that means that someday I can too.

Mom stares out at the mess again, and I notice one stack of boxes in the back corner that is still upright. They probably wouldn't be if Audrey hadn't gotten here when she did.

"You know, there's a lot of stuff in here. Some of these boxes go way, way back. Stuff from Colorado from when he was your age, from high school, college. It's all here when you're ready. I saved it for you and Xan. I know some of it might not make much sense without him here to explain it, and of course I can go through any of it with you."

I didn't know anything in here went that far back. All the way to my age.

"And I know Phil, when you're ready, he wants to be there for you. To help you know those other parts of your dad. Okay?"

"Do you think . . ."

"Yeah?" Mom asks.

"Well, I don't know if he'd want to. He probably still thinks I'm a jerk after how I was when he first came here. Phil, I mean."

Mom's face breaks into a smile, but she fights it. "I think he'll be able to look past that."

29

MOM HEADS INTO THE HOUSE FOR A

dustpan, a broom, and some trash bags, and then we go to town on the shed, trying to get it in decent shape before she has to go pick up Xander.

It seems crazy now that I could have ever believed my real dad was Phil. But I guess I was no different from that baby bird in *Are You My Mother?* So desperately wanting a dad again that I'd take almost anyone.

Though in my defense, at least Phil is the same species as me and not an airplane.

By the time Mom leaves for the Y, the shed looks

sort of okay again. Trash bags filled with old files sit by the door, along with a box full of broken glass because Mom didn't know how to throw out glass, and honestly, I have no idea either. Stacked by the back window are ten boxes of Dad's personal stuff that Mom is going to save for Xander and me. One from elementary school, one from middle school, two from high school, three from college, and three more from later years.

When I peeked inside, there was too much stuff in there to even know where to start. G.I. Joes and baseball cards, playbills and rolled-up posters for bands I've never heard of, heavy plastic envelopes full of photographs, notebooks and papers from school, video games and Hot Wheels, snow globes and cheap plastic souvenirs from trips, comic books and ticket stubs and medals and awards, handwritten letters and tiny folded-up notes on lined paper, school pictures, CD cases and VHS tapes and cassettes, old coins and gemstones and honestly, I think some just straight-up rocks. He held on to all of it. All these years.

I removed one thing from his high school box—his yearbook from senior year—and brought it up to my bedroom, where I lie belly-down on my unmade bed. I crack open the yearbook and flip back to the senior wills, searching for Dad's.

Always remember: Phantom, Nirvana, Red Rocks, NYC, the Crew.

Thanks to: Kayla, for everything.

I search for Mom in the index—Kayla Pinkerton— and turn to the pages that have her. Tennis. French Club. The Literary Club. She wasn't in the same grade as Dad and Phil—she's a year younger, just a junior in this yearbook. Her hair is longer and she has big poufy bangs. It looks weird, but all the other girls had them too then, so maybe everyone thought they looked cool or something?

There's a picture toward the front of the yearbook, taken at homecoming. Mom is dancing with her friends and there's this guy with his hands around her waist who looks like Phil. There's no caption, though, and it's dark in the photo, so I'm not sure.

I go back through all the pages, searching for Dad. It's like Facebook, almost, except Dad was never on it. He thought stuff like that was for people with too much time on their hands. I find him in the cast picture for the spring musical, *Joseph and the Amazing Technicolor Dreamcoat*. Dad was Pharaoh.

But the pictures are only the beginning. Inside the cover and sprinkled all over are notes and signatures scribbled in blue and black ink from dozens—no, maybe a hundred—different people.

I'm so lost in trying to make out someone's illegible handwriting I don't even hear Mom return with Xander until there's a tap on my door. No way Xander's that quiet.

I close the yearbook. "Yeah, Mom?"

"I just ran into Mrs. Nunes while I was grabbing the mail. Anything you want to tell me?"

I flip over, leaning back on my elbows. "I haven't seen Filipe today." It's not a lie. I haven't talked to him in almost a whole week—since last Tuesday.

"I didn't mean about today. She mentioned a scuffle between the two of you last week. That ring a bell?"

"Oh. That."

Mom raises an eyebrow. "Yeah, *that*. What's going on between you two? Any other summer, he'd be over nearly every night. No wonder I haven't needed to buy as much ice cream lately. Drew?"

I shrug.

"It's just me." Her voice is gentle. "You can tell me what's going on, remember?"

I fix my eyes on the part of my rug where Filipe would lay out his sleeping bag those summer nights when he'd had too much of Anibal picking on him and just wanted another place to crash. "I don't know what happened—he just—he doesn't think I'm cool enough to hang out with him anymore."

"Since when is—"

"Mom, stop. You don't know who's cool in my grade, all right?"

"Okay. Well . . . his loss, then. I think you're plenty cool."

"You're my mom. You *have* to think that."

"But what happened? A real fight? You've never . . . you've never hit anyone before."

"And I probably won't again. I sucked at it."

"Drew."

"No, really. Trust me. I think I hurt myself more than I hurt him. Look, no offense, Mom, but you just . . . you'll never really understand *this*. I promise next time I'll tell you, like we said."

"Would you want to talk about it with Mr. Nunes? Or Anibal?"

"*Mom.* Come on. They'll just take his side."

"I don't know. You need to talk to somebody about it."

"Maybe . . ." A week ago, I would've said no way. Just over two weeks ago, I didn't even know the guy. But now, after everything? Phil spent the day exploring Providence, but he's probably wrapping that up soon and coming back this way. At least, I hope. "Is Phil having dinner with us tonight?"

"Actually, he should be here any minute." As Mom stares back at me, I think I catch her eyes tearing up. Just the tiniest bit.

30

"THIS IS DELICIOUS, KAYLA. REALLY,"

Phil says as he slices through a seared scallop.

"All credit to my sous chef." Mom nods my way. "Last week Drew spotted this new David Chang cookbook on display at the library. Good to try new things, right?"

Xander wrinkles his nose. "Not if the new thing smells like pee."

"That was just the fish sauce," I say. "I swear, not one ounce of pee in this recipe."

"Drew!" Mom swats at me playfully.

"You know, Drew," Phil says. "They make—" He stops what he's saying and looks up at me right then. "Never mind."

"No, tell me." With my napkin, I wipe the corner of my mouth.

"I don't want to step on your toes."

"You're not." I smile to let him know I'm serious. That there's no beef between us, no competition in the kitchen anymore. "Just say it."

"There's a type of fish sauce that doesn't have that, ah, how do we say, *eau de urine*." I catch Mom scrunch her nose—probably 'cause she's about had it with our pee talk at dinner. "I'll write it down for you."

"Cool. Thanks."

Mom butts in. "So," she says, raising her fork, "what's the plan for tomorrow?" I steal a peek at her left hand. Her ring finger is bare. But then I notice a new necklace she's wearing. Both rings dangle from the thin gold thread, and somehow that feels right.

"You know, after a year of meandering around the country, I'm ready to take the easiest route home. Zip across I-90 over to 80. Little bit of pretty New England and then a whole lot of corn country."

My brother sighs. "I wish we could have corn instead

of this." He pushes the Brussels sprouts around on his plate. Now, I think spicy roasted Brussels sprouts and scallops are tasty, but I guess I forget he still has the palate of a six-year-old. Which means he'd choose mac and cheese or fish sticks over a four-star meal any day.

"Try another few bites, will you?" Mom says to Xander. "And then you can go play Legos."

With an end in sight, Xander shovels in a few bites and is off running into the living room before Mom can shout, "Wash your hands, please!" She leans back in her seat. "Ooof."

"You two have done enough," Phil says. "Let me do the dishes."

"No, no." Mom stands up and turns on some music. "The dishes are my time to unwind. Kayla's Zen time."

It's just Phil and me now. That first night when he came over for dinner, I couldn't wait to get away from the table. Phil awkwardly folds his napkin as he sets it down. I do the same. "Do you want to come out to the backyard? With me, I mean?" I ask.

"Sure thing."

I wash my hands in the kitchen sink before leading Phil out back. We had dinner on the early side, so it's still plenty light as we step outside.

"So," Phil says, slipping his hands into his front pockets as we slowly shuffle across the lawn.

"Mom told me. I mean, I figured it out. About you and my dad. You were . . . you were friends, right?"

"From birth, practically."

"Like me and Filipe." The dry grass crunches under my feet. "Hold on a sec," I say before sprinting across the yard, grabbing the sprinkler from the side of the house, and setting it in the middle of the lawn. I turn on the spigot by the house and water arcs out of the sprinkler.

"Grass looked okay by Colorado standards," Phil says with a laugh. "Now, Kayla mentioned you do puppet shows at the library. Back when we were growing up, your dad and I were really into the Muppets. Kids still watch the Muppets these days?"

"There was that one movie a few years ago. Mom and I watched it on Netflix."

"'Am I a maaaan or am I a Muppet? Am I a Muppet?'" I can't believe Phil is singing the song from the movie. And in falsetto! Phil laughs at himself. "Sorry, not really much of a singer these days."

"You weren't half-bad," I say. Better than I could do.

"Thanks. That's high praise, actually." Phil clears

his throat. "Your dad, he really idolized Jim Henson. You know who he is, right?"

"He created the Muppets and *Sesame Street*." I open the door to the shed and flip on the overhead light.

Phil stops for a second, taking in everything. We cleaned up the shed pretty good, Mom and me. There's no way he can tell what happened in here earlier today. Unless Mom told him. I search his face for a sign. No, I don't think she did. At least, not yet.

"These boxes in the back have all the stuff from when he was younger." I pull down the top one, labeled *Middle School*, and set it on the floor. "I thought maybe, if it's all right with you, you could, you know . . ." I glance up at him. "Tell me about the stuff. Like, what you remember. Stories about my dad. Not all the boxes tonight or anything. Just to start."

Phil clears his throat again. I think he's tearing up, but maybe it's just all the dust in here. "I'd love that, Drew."

I remove the cover, and for a moment we're just staring at the jumble of items until I make the first move, reaching my hand in there. I pull out one of those thick plastic envelopes from CVS. Inside are dozens of photographs. "Do you know what these are from?" I hand the stack to Phil.

He flips through them, letting me look along with him. A bunch of them are out of focus, a blur of flesh and black. Man, my dad was a terrible photographer back then. "Why are these so blurry?"

"Oh man, Drew. Don't even ask." Phil chuckles. "If I remember correctly, your dad wanted to see if he could take a picture of the inside of his nose."

"What?" That sounds like something Filipe and I would've done.

Finally we flip to a picture that's more obvious: a crisp shot of the Washington Monument.

Phil peers at the photograph. "The eighth-grade class trip!"

"You went to Washington, DC?"

"We fund-raised all year for this. Now, you asked why the photos are so blurry. That's because, shock of all shocks, back then we couldn't see what we were taking a picture of."

"What do you mean? Of course you could see it."

"Nope." Phil laughs, shaking his head. "It's not like it is with your smartphones. Back then you had to put a roll of film into a camera and actually look through the viewfinder. You couldn't zoom or focus. You never really knew how things would turn out until you dropped the film off and got the photos back a few days later."

"That's crazy."

"That's growing up in the nineties for you."

We flip through a bunch of out-of-focus shots, a few photos taken outside the White House, and then we get to one that makes Phil yelp so loud I almost jump. "What?"

"I haven't thought about her in *years*. No—decades." The girl in the picture is off to the side, wearing a big teal-and-purple sweatshirt and braces.

"Who is she?"

"Heather Spencer. The crush to end all crushes. Or so I thought."

I squint to try to see it, but no, that girl just looks weird. "Was there anyone my dad liked? You know, a girl?"

"Oh, believe me. I *know*." Phil flips through the photos again. "Renée Cassidy."

Never heard of her, but I guess that's not a big surprise. "Did she like him back?" Phil throws his head back and laughs. "So no?"

"Well, maybe? Let's just say we never got to the

bottom of that question. Back in seventh grade, Jimmy was way, way too shy to ask a girl out. Not that I didn't try to make him."

"You did? How?"

"This probably sounds like ancient history to you, but back in the nineties, we didn't have Snapchat or Instagram, so it was all about notes. Handwritten notes."

"Like the ones at the bottom of this box?"

"Exactly. You know what? He probably saved some good ones. Luckily for him, Jimmy didn't stay shy forever."

Jimmy. It feels weird to hear him call my dad that. Like he was a whole different person back then. But then, maybe he was.

We finish flipping through that set of pictures. Before I decide on the next thing, I clear my throat. "Can I ask you a question?"

"Sure thing."

"I don't really know how to say this. I mean, it might be rude to ask. . . ."

Phil shakes his head. "Shoot."

"What happened to your brother? He and I, we have the same name, right?"

"You do. Well, he went by Andy."

I repeat the name quietly. "Andy."

"Andy was two years younger than me. He was my shadow, you know? Well, of course you do—you have Xander. Andy died of brain cancer the summer before I started eighth grade."

"I'm so sorry," I say.

"Me too, Drew." Phil runs his hand through his hair. "When you're young and someone dies— especially someone that close to you—it shapes you. I had to grow up real fast. One day I was still a kid and the next, I wasn't, you know?"

The thing is, I do.

"I don't know who I'd be if Andy were still alive."

"You think you'd be different?"

"All the choices I've made since then, I feel like I had to really live my life. Not just be a passenger along for the ride. That's why I traveled for so long. It's why I bike. The bike ride this summer, it was a way to honor Andy's life by raising money for cancer research. There have been a lot of medical advances since Andy died, but we still have a long way to go. This summer is the thirtieth anniversary of his death. Thirty years."

It's only been three years since Dad died. Well, three years, five months, and—counting the days is too hard. Thirty, though. One day it will be thirty years since Dad was gone. That feels like so many.

"Do you think my dad—do you think he named me after him?"

"I'd like to think he did, but to be honest, Drew, I don't know for sure. You could ask your mom, though. Your dad and I hadn't been in touch for so long." Phil takes in a slow breath. "Look, I want you to know, if you ever want to talk about your dad, if you've got questions about anything from back then, anytime, I'm just a phone call or video chat away. For you, and for Xan."

I scan over the boxes in front of me, all of them packed to the brim. Each item with a story, a memory, something about Dad I'd probably never know otherwise. I want to know it all, but it's not something we're going to do tonight and be done with. I'll be unpacking these boxes for weeks, months. Years? I'll be unpacking Dad forever.

I reach in and pull out a small, slightly wrinkled trifold. A playbill for *Aladdin*. "Our first play," Phil says. "Well, just children's community theater. No Broadway for us."

There are signatures—sorry, *autographs*—from the cast members. I open it up, searching for the cast list. "Who was Dad?" I ask. But before Phil answers, I see it. He was Aladdin.

"The man, the myth, the legend. Aladdin himself."

"Wait, and who were you?" I have to keep going down the list a while until I see Phil Pittman listed. *Street urchin.*

"I was more of a behind-the-scenes guy, to be honest. Loved making the sets, plus hanging out with everyone."

My dad was the star. "How about my dad?"

"Well, I'm not sure Jimmy always believed in himself, which is crazy to think about because he was talented. He could sing and act, the whole package. Well, minus the dancing. Oof. He sure could test the choreographer. No, your dad had this special charisma. You couldn't not watch Jimmy McCormack onstage. But even offstage, at least then, he had this nervous energy about him. I think that's true of a lot of actors."

My eyes smart for a second. I wish I could see it, that I could've been there somehow to see that version of my dad.

"You know, he's probably got a recording some-where." Phil digs through the box a little. "Yup!" He pulls out a VHS tape with *Aladdin* written on the yellowed tape down the side.

"I don't think my mom has anything that can play it."

"Oh, there are plenty of old VCRs floating around. I'm sure Kay can track one down on Craigslist for you."

I'd be able to see him. The real him. Jimmy McCormack, back when he was my age. But am I ready?

I put the VHS tape back in the box for now and glance out the window. The sun's almost set, and I really should move the sprinkler to a new spot so that it soaks the whole yard. But there's one thing I still have to ask Phil about.

"Did you and my dad ever have fights? Like, when you were my age, I mean."

"Yeah, of course. We butted heads about all kinds of things."

"No—" I shake my head. "A real fight."

"Jimmy wasn't much for confrontation. And I usually tried to keep the peace too. But, you know, even if it feels like it's been a while, it's never too late to say you're sorry."

"Even if the other person started it?"

"You need to ask yourself what's important to you. And if that friendship is important to you, then you do what it takes to make things right. Apologize, but don't be afraid to explain why what your friend did was hurtful. You need to be able to have a real back-and-forth. That's what makes a good friendship after all, right? Honesty."

I haven't exactly been super honest with Filipe lately.

"Do you wish you and my dad had stayed friends?"

"Let's put it this way: I sure wish I hadn't thrown away all those years of friendship over a girl."

"Hey," I say, suddenly realizing what he's saying. "That's my mom you're talking about."

Phil laughs. "I know. But you understand the sentiment, right? We should've been able to get past that. At least, *I* should have." He glances out the window. "You know, it's been a real trip these past few weeks, getting to spend time with you and your brother. Jimmy's boys." He shakes his head like it's hard to believe that the person he knew as a kid could have ever grown up to be a dad. To be my dad.

And then he goes quiet for a second, and I wonder what other thoughts are running through his head.

When he and my dad were my age, did they ever imagine this far out?

Phil sniffles and runs his hand through his hair. "If only I'd been around. If I hadn't been so far away. If I'd just stayed in touch." He lets out a sigh and then turns back to me. "You know, you and Xander remind me so much of Jimmy. Both of you. You've got his smile and that creative streak, Xan's got his sense of humor and, I swear, the exact same cowlick. There's more, of course. You got different parts of him . . . the best parts."

I'd never thought of it that way before. Assumed being Dad's son was an all-or-nothing deal, but it's not. Of course it isn't. He had good parts and bad parts like anyone else. It's just, ever since he died, it felt like the bad parts overwhelmed the good ones.

Just then the outside lights turn on and my mom steps out onto the deck. "Xander's demanding a bedtime story and says I don't do it right. Any takers?"

I put the top on the box. As Phil and I step out into the yard, I hear the faint *bop-bop* of a basketball across the street. Phil and I eye each other. "You know what, you should take a stab at it," I say. "But get ready, because Xan's got some high standards."

MAYBE I WOULDN'T FEEL COMFORTABLE

heading over in the middle of the afternoon knowing Theo could be there—wouldn't want to get in the way of *one-on-one* again—but at almost nine o'clock on a Tuesday night, I can almost guarantee it's only Filipe just out of sight on the other side of the bushes.

He takes a shot, the ball bouncing off the rim, but then he makes it in on a rebound. I'm standing in the shadows, trying to find the right moment to let him know I'm there, when he turns his head real fast and ducks in surprise. "You reenacting a slasher movie?"

"No," I say. "Sorry—I didn't want to mess with your shot."

He holds up the ball. "You want to play?"

"Sure."

He bounces it my way and I dribble it a little while, warming myself up before I take a shot. *Swoosh*. Not bad. Filipe jogs in and grabs it, taking it back beyond where the arc would be to shoot a three. *Swish*.

"Nice one."

Filipe shrugs, just standing there, bouncing the ball in place. I know I need to say something about what happened a week ago, but it's not as easy as Phil made it out to be. Where do I even start?

"Hey, can we talk?"

"Fine." Filipe takes a shot, the ball bouncing off the rim. Neither of us goes to get it. Our eyes follow as it rolls over to the garage door, finally coming to a stop.

"Look," I say, not sure what's going to come out next. "I'm sorry about last week—the fight—but the thing is, it's been weird ever since you got back from soccer camp, and I don't get it. I don't get what's changed."

"Nothing's *changed*," Filipe says.

I eyeball him.

"Does it need to be that big a deal if I want to hang out with other people sometimes? I mean, you didn't exactly seem happy when me and Theo came by the library."

"That's not true. I was just—"

"Surprised that I would ever come to your *special* place? Interrupt things between you and—what's her name—Audrey? You said she drove you nuts. Didn't look like that, though. You didn't even introduce us to her."

Did he really feel that way? Was it possible that Filipe felt as rejected as I did? "Did you really want me to?"

Filipe shrugs. "Kind of. You're there so much of the time, Drew. I mean, fine, if she really is the worst thing ever, I guess I don't need to meet her. But it didn't look that way when we were there."

"Wait a sec. So it's my fault for not introducing you to Audrey but it's totally cool for you to boot me from shooting hoops with you and Theo?"

Filipe's mouth opens and shuts.

"How would you feel if some random guy who's interested in *your* mom had come over to your house and all you wanted was to get away from him for a few minutes but your friend booted you because he's got a new friend who's older and cooler than you?"

"Like crap," Filipe says. Behind his eyes, I can almost see it clicking into place as he swaps out his POV for mine. Maybe we all need to do that a little more often. "I'm sorry," he says. "I was being a jerk. And I'm sorry for earlier, for picking on you about your mom and that guy. But why didn't you just say something? You never talk about your dad anymore. And I get it—no, that's wrong. I don't get it. We're not little kids, Drew. You're my best friend. You're *supposed* to tell me stuff." He sounds surprisingly frustrated. "You still think about him, right? I mean, you must, because I do."

"You do?"

"Of course. He was your *dad*, Drew. I spent a lot of time with him too. But how come you never talk about him anymore?"

I guess part of me thought Chad's House was the spot to talk about Dad. And so I did. But when that ended—well, Filipe's right. I don't talk about my dad with him. At least, I haven't for a long time.

"Drew?"

"I don't know why," I begin to say. The thing is, suddenly I get what's been wrong with Filipe and me. It wasn't just about him becoming friends with Theo—not really. It was me. And the elephant in the room. "I want to, though. I guess maybe I thought it would weird you out or . . ."

"It won't."

For a second, all I can hear is the croaking of some nearby frogs. "You weren't exactly wrong about the guy on the motorcycle," I say. It's a start.

"Wait, really?" Filipe jogs over for the ball and bounce-passes it to me. "I saw his motorcycle come back the other day. Is it weird with him?"

"Not as much as at first."

"But he's not your dad."

"I know." Maybe someday I'll tell Filipe how I thought he could be. But for now I leave it at that. "He's not trying to be. And anyway, he's leaving tomorrow. Going back to Colorado."

"So it's over?"

"I don't know, actually." This time, it's the truth. I need to ask Mom. Maybe she doesn't even know, but it sure seems like they're planning to stay in touch between now and next summer. "Hey, can you pass me the ball?" I jog over to the far side of his driveway. "I want to take a crazy shot."

If there were such a thing, this shot would be a six-pointer. It's got to be three car lengths from the hoop, minimum.

"No way are you making that in." Filipe laughs.

"Yeah, but what if I do?"

"If you do—um . . . If you do, I'll give you all the money in my bank account."

"You would not."

"I know!" Filipe smiles. "But you're not going to make that shot, so it doesn't matter."

"Okay." Honestly, the basket is so far away that the only chance I have of making it in—and we're talking infinitesimally small chance—is if I take a total granny shot. "For all the money in your bank account. One, two, three."

I fling the ball up toward the basket. It's still arcing up. Now it's coming down. Oh my God, it's close. It's—

"Off the rim! Are you kidding me?" Filipe's mouth is wide open, like he can't believe it either.

I'm legit falling over laughing, a borderline pee-my-pants situation.

Filipe goes after the ball and dribbles it back toward me. "Crap, that was close."

"Yeah," I say, holding my fingers a centimeter apart. "I was this close to being rich."

"You have unrealistic expectations about my bank account." Filipe laughs.

Across the street, the light is still on in Xander's room. I wonder how Phil's making out with the bedtime story. Xan's probably hassling him for not creating unique enough voices for each character the way I do. "I should head back and say good night to Xan."

"Okay, yeah."

I'm heading down the driveway when Filipe yells out my name. "Yeah?" I say back, turning around. He's jogging toward me.

"Are we cool again?"

"Yeah," I say. "Of course we're cool. Later, Filipe."

"Night, Drew."

The sky's clear tonight and the chrome on Phil's motorcycle reflects the moonlight. Tomorrow morning he'll be on that thing, zooming down our road for the last time for a while. After how much has happened in the last few weeks, I can't honestly imagine how much will change by the time he comes back next summer. Assuming he does, that is. Next summer I'll be a page-in-training. Hopefully Audrey will too. Mom's she shed will finally be finished. And Xan will be seven and a quarter, so watch out, world.

Right then my phone buzzes. I expect it to be Filipe now that things are cool again, but it's not. It's from Audrey. A photo of a chicken—the kind we saw at the county fair, the white Silkie bantam.

My parents said yes! I'm getting TWO chickens!

She sends me a GIF of someone doing a happy dance.

Can you help me name them?

Sure, I text back, thinking about the long list of names she came up with for our fake patron and how she probably doesn't *need* my help. It's sure going to be interesting when Mom talks to Loretta tomorrow.

Through the open window upstairs, I can hear Phil reading Xander his bedtime story. Every now and then Xander groans. "You're not doing it right," he says. "Drew does it better." And then Phil tries again.

"Oh, you guys." Mom's laughter. "Let's wrap it up. The rest of us have to go to sleep someday."

I head inside through the garage.

"Finally!" Xan shouts as I close the door behind me. "Drew's back. Drew, can you finish the story? Sorry, but Phil's not as good at it as you are."

"Xan!" Mom snaps. "Where are your manners?"

"Okay, okay!" I shout back, slipping off my shoes. "I'll be right there."

When I get to my brother's room, Phil hands me *Bread and Jam for Frances*. "Wow, you weren't kidding," Phil says.

"Much better." Xan settles under his covers with his stuffies lined up next to him in bed. "Okay, actually, can you start from the beginning?"

"Sure, Xan." I squeeze onto the bed beside him, my back up against the headboard, and in my very best spoiled badger voice, I begin to read.

AUTHOR'S NOTE

More than a decade ago, when I was finishing up my library science degree at Simmons College, I completed an independent study project at the Children's Room, a grief support center for children and teenagers in Arlington, Massachusetts. I helped them devise a system for cataloging their extensive collection, which included many novels about children experiencing grief. It was essential, the staff noted, for the children to see their own experiences mirrored in fiction and nonfiction.

Though recently there have been more public conversations around mental illness and suicide, the stigma still remains. Like Drew, so many feel afraid or uncomfortable talking about suicide. But not talking about difficult subjects doesn't make them go away. It just makes those dealing with them feel more alone.

As of the time this book went into print, suicide is the second-leading cause of death among individuals between the ages of ten and thirty-four. According to the 2017 CDC report, suicide annually claims the lives of over forty-seven thousand Americans. If you have lost a friend or a loved one to suicide, I want you to know that you are not alone. There are countless people out there who understand what you are going through, as well as trained professionals who want to help.

If you or someone you know would like to talk with a licensed mental health professional, consider reaching out to a therapist through:

American Association for Marriage and Family Therapy:
aamft.org

American Counseling Association:
counseling.org

American Mental Health Counselors Association:
amhca.org

American Psychological Association:
apa.org

National Association of Social Workers:
socialworkers.org

FURTHER RESOURCES

National Suicide Prevention Lifeline

suicidepreventionlifeline.org

This national network of crisis centers offers free emotional support 24-7, including specific resources for kids. Call 1-800-273-TALK (8255).

Crisis Text Line

The free, 24-7 confidential text message service for people in crisis. Text HOME to 741741 in the United States.

American Association for Suicidology

suicidology.org

This nonprofit organization advocates for suicide prevention and envisions a world where people know how to prevent suicide and find hope and healing.

American Foundation for Suicide Prevention

afsp.org

AFSP is the nation's largest nonprofit dedicated to saving lives and bringing hope to those affected by suicide.

The Dougy Center

dougy.org

The Portland, Oregon–based National Center for Grieving Children & Families provides support in a safe place for children, teens, young adults, and their families grieving a death to share their experiences.

Eluna

elunanetwork.org

Eluna offers resources and programs—including camps—to address the needs of children experiencing confusing emotions in the wake of a loved one's death or addiction.

National Alliance for Grieving Children

childrengrieve.org

This professional member organization specifically addresses issues about child bereavement and offers continuing education, peer networking, and a national database of children's bereavement support programs.

Suicide Awareness Voices of Education

save.org

SAVE's mission is to prevent suicide through public awareness and education, to reduce stigma, and to serve as a resource for those touched by suicide.

ACKNOWLEDGMENTS

This book would not exist if not for the profound influence of libraries and librarians on my life. Mrs. Littlejohn, my elementary school librarian, and Dawn Clarke, the children's librarian at Joshua Hyde Public Library, who gave me my first-ever job as her assistant, created safe spaces for me and countless other children over the years.

My first career was as a teen librarian in the suburbs of Chicago and Boston, where it was my daily work to create a haven for today's tweens and teens. The teenagers who attended my programs over the years and found a second home in the library continue to inspire my writing to this day. To my once and forever librarian colleagues who champion literacy and are on the front lines providing vital services for communities across the country, I am in awe of you. You don't get nearly enough credit for the work you do.

I couldn't be luckier than to land in Cincinnati with its enviable library system. The staff at the Oakley Branch Library in particular is fantastic. They've never once made me feel embarrassed about the exorbitant number of books I check out every week. Even when I walk home with both a backpack *and* a tote bag full of books.

As much as I don't know where I'd be without libraries, I can't begin to imagine the journey of writing this book without those who have been there through the ups and downs. I'm forever grateful to my agent, Katie Grimm, who continues to push me (and forces me to outline, even when I'd rather recklessly continue to pants my way through each draft). There's no one else I'd rather have in my corner. Special thanks to her then-assistant, Cara Bellucci, for her thoughtful reads. With the sound guidance of Tricia Lin and Alyson Heller, Drew's story became ever so more layered and nuanced. I'm so grateful for them and the entire team at Aladdin. Thank you, too, to Julie McLaughlin, for your beautiful cover illustration, which perfectly captures Drew's perceived distance from his peers.

As this book inched its way along, I count myself fortunate to have received thoughtful reads from writer friends Anne Bowen, Melanie Conklin, Kelly Dyksterhouse, Stephanie Farrow, Autumn Krause, Robin Kirk, Jonathan Lenore Kastin, Jennifer Maschari, Ellen Reagan, Shelley Saposnik, and C. M. Surrisi. Extra thanks to Abby Cooper for being a wise owl when I need it. Tawoo, tawoo! And for all my Facebook friends who chime in on my hive mind posts: you are the only reason I am still on Facebook these days. Thanks for doing me a solid again and again. That 1990s ephemera brainstorm session was a delight.

I'm ever appreciative of the friends and family who have supported my writing and publishing efforts over the years. To my parents, my husband, my brother, and all of my extended family: thank you! I promise none of the antagonists in my books will ever be based on you.

Drew's story strays far from my personal experience—I've neither experienced life as a twelve-year-old boy, nor have I lost a close family member to suicide—and as such, it required research. Along the way, I found insight in the following books: *Masterminds and Wingmen* by Rosalind Wiseman, *Raising Cain* by Dan Kindlon and Michael Thompson, *After a Parent's Suicide* by Margo Requarth, and *Breaking the Silence* by Linda Goldman. As a mental health professional, Rose Kormanyos provided a helpful read on the late-stage manuscript. Any mistakes or misunderstandings of Drew's experience are my own.

Every day I'm reminded that writing for young readers is an enormous privilege. For as long as I get to do this, I'm grateful for each and every reader my books find.

ABOUT THE AUTHOR

Jenn Bishop is the author of the middle-grade novels *14 Hollow Road* and *The Distance to Home*, which was a Junior Library Guild selection, a Bank Street College Best Children's Book, and an Amazon.com Editor's Pick. She grew up in New England, where she fell in love with the ocean, Del's frozen lemonade, and the Boston Red Sox before escaping to college at the University of Chicago. After working as a teen and children's librarian, she received her MFA in writing for children and young adults from Vermont College of Fine Arts. Jenn currently calls Cincinnati, Ohio, home. Visit her online at jennbishop.com.